NEW YEARS
TO
CHRISTMAS:
FIFTEEN
QUEER
HOLIDAY
TALES

doorQ Publishing | Playa del Rey, California

Published in the USA by
doorQ Publishing
8675 Falmouth Ave #306
Playa del Rey, CA 90293
www.doorq.com

Item no. DQP-FICN-1004

ISBN-10: 0615733301
ISBN-13: 978-0615733302

Cover Model: Clayton Doyle
Photography: Tania R. Williams
Back Cover Art: Jon Macy

Printed in the United States of America

TABLE OF CONTENTS

For Joseph, who makes every day a holiday.

FOREWORD

In December 2011, I was invited to be a part of a gay short story reading. Because of the month involved, the person coordinating the event, a very sweet gentleman by the name of Hank Henderson, requested that each new spoken story be Christmas themed. What came out of this was the final story of this book, "Christmas in the City".

A month after the reading, I became a bit twitchy. For some reason, I just couldn't leave the story be. I felt as if I were leaving a brand new creation to sit and collect dust on a shelf. Inspired by the holiday bug, I decided to create a new book project incorporating my earlier Christmas season tale plus so much more.

Personally, I've always been a huge fan of all the holidays. The prospect of engaging in each ritual, dressing up for each occasion, decking out the homestead accordingly, buying beautifully colored greeting cards...well, they always held a bit of childhood magic for me. Because of this, I decided to give a little honor to several other festive American holidays celebrated throughout the year for this book project.

When it comes to the holidays, gay culture does add a unique spin to the different occasions altogether. Holidays like Halloween and Marti Gras take on an entirely new fun gay life of their own in the larger metropolitan areas. I'm so thankful that we've come such a long way in just a few short decades. After all, it wasn't that long ago that the now long closed Black Cat Tavern in the Silver Lake neighborhood of Los Angeles was raided by police one New Year's evening simply because the patrons there kissed each other at the stroke of midnight to celebrate the occasion. What started out as an innocent holiday tradition quickly transformed into beatings and warrantless arrests. Two years later, the Stonewall riots in New York City would help change that injustice, eventually helping to bring about a more socially balanced outlook we can thankfully enjoy today.

That said, despite having a more comfortable environment to be ourselves in (*i.e.* marriage, job security and being visible in general), we still have a long way to go. This still includes how we celebrate holidays. Each year, LGBT people are repeatedly excluded from the New York City St. Patrick's Day parade. They are instead forced to celebrate the occasion in the far less hostile neighborhood of Queens. (*how apropos*) Yet, other gay people find themselves rejected from the families they were born into and instead are left to create their own self-made families to capture that holiday spirit they had in days gone by. It's with these people and struggles in mind that I hope this book captures some attention and brings a little honorable memory to.

I'm also very honored to include the artwork of the ever-talented Jon Macy as part of this book project. Anyone familiar with gay comic art from the 1990s and onward has undoubtedly heard of this amazing gentleman. Winner of the prestigious Lambda Literary Award for his illustrated book *Teleny and Camille*, Mr. Macy is an excellent professional whose talent is a treasured asset to the gay community and art world in general.

Two additional '*holidays*' in the book you'll notice, though, are listed due to being honorary days of gay appreciation: Academy Award night and Tony Award night. They're both labeled 'gay night of nights' for a reason after all, so they made the cut.

As with my previously released *Queer Tales: A Fantasy Anthology* book, I felt my new holiday project was just the right opportunity to highlight several other friends' and acquaintances' writing talents as well. Please do keep an eye out for future projects written by these incredibly talented individuals. I'm very proud and honored to be able to have each of their works highlighted for you to discover, or in some cases add to your already existing collection of their works.

And with that, voilà! I present to you the fruit of that endeavor. I hope you enjoy each holiday story as much as I and the other writers have enjoyed writing them for you.

Happy holidays everyone!

Peter Saenz
August 2012

JANUARY

NEW YEARS:
"GAY NEW YEAR"
BY PETER SAENZ

The clock on the wall says 10:00pm. PERFECT! I'm not ready. If you've known any fabulously accessorized queen in your life, then you also know that not being ready for a New Year's Eve party at 10:00pm just simply will not do. Blake is gonna kill me.

Pull yourself together Mary. Scratch that. Pull yourself together DIVINA!

That's right. I'm a drag queen. By day I'm a well put together accountant for a large law firm in one of those ridiculously large skyscrapers downtown. I wear Armani suits, carry around an $800 leather briefcase, and tell big shot executives exactly what they can and cannot spend money on daily. When the sun goes down though, that's when the claws come out. Jungle red! Out goes hard ass business man Monty Green, and in comes Divina, the sexiest woman alive. Well, the sexiest woman alive in Milwaukee anyway. Don't judge.

As soon as I strategically fit the last of my bits and pieces into place, I step into my fabulous frock for the night. Once I zip up the back, the revealing flame colored dress I see staring back at me in the full length mirror goes from being a bit too snug to ooo-girl tight. Fierce. Then after slipping on my black thigh high boots, I stand and take one last look at the final ensemble. Girl, there is no way I'll be able to rock these kicks all night, but hey, that's what bar stools are for. Always remember, when it comes to style versus comfort, 'beauty is pain' and well worth it.

I finger tease my hair one last time in the hallway mirror and grab my bedazzled Wonder Woman clutch before strutting out the door and into my awaiting chariot: a red Mazda Miata with a license plate that reads 'Bad Girl'. Again, don't judge.

Before I know it, I'm at Walker's Point and parked in front of Club Boylicious. Girlfriend, if these walls could talk. The club valet speeds off with my ride, leaving me behind to be greeted with cat calls and whistles as I saunter through the front door. The bouncer slaps my ass, to which I dramatically gasp open mouthed with a false sense of modesty.

"Well, I never!" I exclaim.

"Not in the last hour anyway." the tall piece of chocolate winks back at me.

I coo my approval at the truthful words and make my way into the bar. A swarm of 'hey girl' and 'werk' comments of approval fill my jewel dangled ears before I finally reach the nearest drink slinger. It's Derek. His sinewy nude chest is covered in a neatly manscaped fur. His green eyes lock on me and suddenly I'm a high school cheerleader drooling over the star quarter back with one seriously cute tight end.

FYI: NEVER date a co-worker. If it ends badly, there you are, stuck seeing each other night after night. It's not pretty. Never-ending flirtation on the other hand…now THAT I can manage.

Cooing as I sit on the barstool, I ask for my usual drink. Derek mixes a series of alcoholic potions together and places a beautifully full cocktail in front of me. I grab the lime wedge from the rim of my glass and flirtatiously suck on it, smiling seductively at the gorgeous piece of meat in front of me.

"You always service me well," I say in my best Marilyn Monroe voice. I make sure to throw in my trademark wink for added sparkle.

Smiling back, Derek says, "Blake's been looking for you. He's upstairs giving Majenta the riot act."

Rolling my eyes, I reply in my regular voice, "That tired queen deserves every bit of everything she's getting. Did you see how she stole my bit last week? It's only drag, but honey, trash doesn't compete with class."

I push up my fake boobs for dramatic effect, grab my cocktail, and head for the stairs along the far wall. Once I arrive on top (mm-hmm) I open the door to see Blake standing over a very annoyed looking Majenta, sitting in her chair and applying her 12th layer of what appears to be orange cake batter make-up.

In a tone walking a fine line between controlled anger and sudden outburst, Blake says to Majenta, "And what's this I hear about you stealing other performer's tips?"

Sarcastically turning back to Blake, Majenta says in a deep voice, "Prove it."

Ooo girl, this conversation is a bit too heavy for me. I walk over to the other side of the room where I see my other fellow performers, half primping their hair in a separate row of mirrors and half listening in to Majenta's interrogation.

"Hey Ms. Pauletta", I say to the zoftig black girl in the purple sequined dress.

"Mmm-hmm", she replies back, not paying attention to me; obviously too engrossed with what's going on behind us. Now closer to the make-up vanity stations, I can see every queen there using the mirrors to watch what Blake and Majenta will do next.

Noticing that the queen at the far end is about to tip over from ear strain, I bump her back into an upright position with my firm yet beautifully feminine padded hip.

"Careful Cha-Cha, you almost fell on your cojones."

Mumbling something in Spanish under her breath, Cha-Cha adjusts her outfit then leans back again to listen in ala Gladys Kravitz.

Now raising his voice, Blake yells to Majenta, "And I better not hear one more word about any of your drama in the club or you can start looking for someplace else to work!" Grabbing the door handle to go downstairs, Blake turns back and yells, "Divina! You're late!"

Slamming the door behind him, the room instantly becomes a bee hive of murmurs. Thirty seconds into it Majenta turns to the lot of us. "If you bitches have something to say, say it to my face."

The room goes quiet as everyone looks around to see if anyone is fool hearted enough to accept her challenge. Frankly speaking, the troop of girls are a barrel of laughs to perform with, but when it comes to awkward situations they typically leave their spines at the door.

With cocktail in hand, I saunter over to Majenta and take in her full measure. The queens behind me gasp in anticipation.

"I think everything Blake went over with you pretty much sums it up." I smack my lips together, emphasizing the final P for added effect.

Boiling with rage, Majenta stands up and gets in my face.

"Oh yeah, and what are you gonna do about it?"

Leaving only an inch of space between my face and hers, I lean in closer and reply, "I got that covered."

Before I know it, Ms. Pauletta is suddenly between us and catching Majenta's raised hand before it could come down in my general direction.

"Uh-uh", Ms. Pauletta advises. "We ain't gonna have NONE of that around here."

Majenta jerks her hand back, eyeing me in contempt. I smile right back at her, sipping from the straw protruding from my cocktail.

A knock at the door snaps our attention. Willie, the club assistant, pokes his head through the door.

"Majenta, you're on in 5."

He then disappears; completely unaware of the girl fight he almost stumbled into.

Majenta says to me, "This ain't over Divina."

Now grimacing at her, I answer, "Your tone seems very pointed."

With a look as if daggers are about to come flying out of her eyeballs, Majenta turns and leaves the room. She slams the door behind her to let us know just how angry her tired ass is.

Artemis immediately breaks the ice.

"Ooo girl, if you're not careful, one of these days that mouth of yours is gonna write a check it can't cash."

Rolling my eyes, I walk over to Majenta's mirror and inspect my make-up. Wiping some excess lipstick off the corners of my mouth I answer back, "Puh-lease girl. I date rough neck bodybuilders. One ugly gorilla doesn't scare me."

The other queens giggle like school girls.

"Besides, that tired ho is one sneeze away from being fired. She'll probably be working at Maude's next week, shaking her ass for quarters."

Cha-Cha says, "I hope so. When I went to the ladies room last week I came back and found half of my tip money gone from my purse. She says she didn't take it but she was the only one there."

Casta Spella then says, "Did you see those new Iron Fist pumps she was sporting? Say hello to your money honey."

As Cha-Cha goes off in a tirade of Spanish, I cut through it saying, "It's New Year's girls. It's a fresh start for all of us. Off with the old and on with the new. I'm gonna party hardy tonight and I'm not about to let some man in a dress ruin my night."

Ms. Pauletta raises her hand, which I slap in mid-air.

"Yes honey, I heard that!"

The rest of the night is a whirlwind of fun. Once Majenta's totally wrong Lady Gaga performance is over, Ms. Pauletta lets the audience have it with a strong Beyonce' number. Artemis gives some fierce 80s mega-mix realness. Cha-Cha let her sexy out to a hard hitting J.Lo dance song. Casta Spella put everyone under her thrall with a Siouxsie and the Banshees mix. And I'll be damned if I didn't make three times what I usually do performing a number I can only describe as Angelina Jolie meets Tina Turner. What? It could happen.

After the show, the lot of us mingle with the audience. I get bombarded with compliments and even a few gropes. My audience never disappoints. As the evening gets closer to midnight, the club seems to be filling with more hot gay boys than I know what to do with. Completely ravished by my beauty, I lose count of the amounts of drinks bought for me by my adoring fans. I think the amount of alcohol I consumed may have been a contributing factor for what happened next.

A few minutes before midnight, out of the corner of my eye I see a lighted sparkler being waved around in the outside club patio. Call me crazy, but what I 'thought' would be a funny idea jumped into my mind and a plot was soon hatched.

Cat-like in my moves, as always, I slink over to the open patio area and whisper into Mr. Sparkler's ear.

"Got an extra sparkler for a lonely beauty queen?"

The adorable gay boy turns around, confused by the question. His face lights up once he sees who I am. How cute.

"Divina! Oh wow. I loved your performance tonight. You're my favorite girl in the group."

Blushing, I softly thump my fingers on his nicely defined chest saying, "Stop! Lil' ol' me? Why, you're as sweet as can be."

Laughing, the now cuter gay boy says, "I'm Mark. You want a sparkler? I've been passing them out all night. You just can't light them inside the bar."

"Hi Mark. I'd love a sparkler. I'll be sure not to. Thanks hun! It was lovely meeting you."

I sassily grab the offered sparkler, give Mark a kiss on the cheek, and turn back into the bar.

My lovely lashed eyes scan the room until I spot the cow I'm looking for. Standing on the other side of the room, I see Majenta holding court. Flocked by her usual lumpy fans, she's too engrossed to notice me shimmy myself behind the curtains masking the wall behind her. I know I've lined myself directly behind her once I'm able to listen in on her conversation with pin point clarity.

"And then that she-man got in my face trying to read me about how shady I was. I was ready to clock that bitch but 'ol rotund over there stopped me before I could get any licks in. If she thinks this is over, then she's got another thing coming. After midnight I'm going into the parking lot and slashing that bitch's tires. 'I got that covered'. Humph. I got it covered too bitch."

As her homely friends laugh, snicker, and generally encourage Majenta's low class upbringing, I feel for the matches I previously stashed in my ample bosom. With my tools in hand, I patiently wait for the next few minutes to end before the crowd finally is quieted for the customary 10 second countdown to New Years.

Once the roar of '10' is heard, I slit the curtains open to see all eyes are on stage where Blake is holding a cocktail and surrounded by the club go-go boys waiting to blow into their noise makers.

'9'. Directly in front of me is Majenta's back. She is sitting her fat ass on a stool, too downtrodden by her ass's girth to stand. Perfect.

'8'. I slip the handle end of my sparkler between Majenta's bull sized buns and the straining stool seat beneath them.

'7'. I take a match and strike it against the rough black strip along the matchbox side.

'6'. The match light burns.

'5'. I push the flame against the now jutting sparkler.

'4'. The sparkler begins to spark, so I shake the match to extinguish the flame.

'3'. I shimmy as fast as I can along the wall back towards the bar, still hidden by the black curtains covering it.

'2'. I finally reach the end of the curtain and peek around to see if anyone is there. Thankfully all eyes are still facing the stage.

'1'. I slip out of the curtain and put my arm around sparkler guy Mark, who I see next to me. He turns to see who I am and smiles another great big smile in my direction.

'Happy New Year!!!"

As I discreetly put the now extinguished match into my clutch, the room becomes a loud celebration of noise makers, cheers, hugs, kisses, and wild abandonment. Mark surprises me with a very affectionate hug, which I happily give back. I flick my head back towards the bar and see stud-muffin Derek wink at me in admiration.

Suddenly I hear a very loud scream. Everyone in the bar turns to look at who's making the commotion.

Running around in a circle, Majenta is yelling bloody murder. Now in an open space of her own, she spins around madly, flailing her arms in the air. As if they were trained to do so all their lives, the club instantly becomes a sea of lit cell phones recording the incident in question.

Once Majenta spins around a final time, I see her back and notice that it looks as if her asshole is shooting flames. I guess the end of the sparkler snagged into her rag of a dress. Screaming at the top of her lungs, she yells "Help me! Help me!"

One of her more dull minded friends, in a spurt of unbridled genius, takes his drink and flings it at the flame hoping to extinguish the fire. The alcohol of his drink however does anything but, instead making the flame grow three times instantly. The polyester blend fabric of Majenta's second hand couture dress, now doused with alcohol, soon catches fire as well. So instead of just her asshole shooting flames, her whole hippo sized ass becomes a towering inferno.

"My ass is on fire! My ass is on fire!"

Like a hero out of the blue, Derek the bartender appears with a fire extinguisher in hand and makes short work of the flames on Majenta's car sized rump.

"My ass! My ass!"

When the cold white fire extinguisher mist finally evaporates, we see the remnants of Majenta's titanic sized bottom. Where once there was her 'girl ass' now stands a black, charred, and generally dilapidated mess of foam padding jutting out of the derriere portion of Majenta's dress. The now doused sparkler, still snagged into the padding, lies downward limply, like a sad tail.

Blake, pushing his way through the throngs of party goers, reaches Majenta and asks, "What the hell just happened?"

With eyes aflame, Majenta says, "Someone just lit me on fire you no good lazy sack of shit!"

Inspecting Majenta's now half there fat bottom, Blake asks, "Are you alright? Were you burned?"

"Does it LOOK like I was burned!? My dress is ruined! God damn it, who did it!? WHO DID IT!?"

Manically, Majenta begins grabbing at people near her, shaking them repeatedly.

"Did you do this to me!? Did you? Did you set me on fire!? When I find out who did it, I'm gonna kill them!"

Seeing the situation for what it is, Blake immediately pulls Majenta away from the innocent yet now physically shaken onlookers / videographers.

"What in the hell are you doing!? You don't know that any of these people did anything to you!"

Pushing Blake away to release his hold, Majenta gets a solid stance before she slaps Blake across his cheek. As if the drag gods were smiling upon us, two tank sized police officers appear out of nowhere. They stand directly in front of Majenta, blocking any further access to Blake or other new potential victims to her wrath.

"What's going on here?" The look on the police officer says in no uncertain terms that he isn't fooling around. "Why did you just strike this man?"

Livid, Majenta says, "He put his hands on me."

The more approachable police officer turns to Blake and asks, "Is this true?"

Holding the new red marked cheek with a hand of his own, Blake replies, "It's true. I'm the owner of this club and I was trying to get her to stop manhandling my guests."

Another of Majenta's attack victims, a cute lesbian, speaks up. "She did attack us. I have it filmed on my camera phone if you'd care to see it."

Yet another victim confirms, "You can see it happen on my phone too."

Suddenly a plethora of people extend their phones to the two officers as proof of Majenta's mania. I'm internally gagging from excitement.

Realizing that she's now up shit's creek; Majenta screams, "But they set me on fire! Look at my ass! Look at what they did to me!"

The stern officer asks Majenta, "Did you see any of them do it?"

Fuming, Majenta shouts, "No, but they HAD to have! One of these twisted mother fuckers set my ass on fire!"

Raising his hands in the air, the stern policeman tells Majenta to calm down. This only triggers a higher level of Majenta's intense rage issues. Her wild eyes dart around the room until she finally gets a good view of Blake again. A primal scream erupts in what I'm sure is Majenta's free clinic needed throat. She charges at Blake as if she is about to choke him to death for some perceived transgression.

The two officers move like lightning, grabbing Majenta's arms and pinning her down to the ground in restraint. Sounding like a cat in the throes of heat, the screams and growls Majenta emanates can be heard two blocks down. As the police officers handcuff Majenta by the hooves, Blake tells them that he wants to press assault charges, both on him and on behalf of the various patrons she manhandled.

As the stronger, more stern officer lifts Majenta to her feet, the softer officer picks up Majenta's purse from the floor.

"Check and see if she has any I.D."

When the officer opens Majenta's purse they are shocked to see several men's wallets inside.

Dumbfounded, Blake says, "What the hell?!"

One person from the club shouts, "Hey! My wallet is missing!"

Another person shouts, "Mine too!"

Soon a small crowd of people are shouting the same sentiments. Who knew?

The stern officer turns to Blake and says, "We're gonna need you to come down with us to make a statement. Same for those of you who were attacked and had your wallets stolen."

Nodding, Blake says, "Of course officer."

Realizing that he's leaving the club in such an awful state, Blake then announces, "I apologize for all of this. A round of drinks for everyone at the bar, compliments of Club Boylicious!"

The club becomes a roar of cheers of approval.

As the officers radio in their pending arrival to the station operator via their shoulder mounted walkie-talkies, Majenta looks at me with the coldest look yet. I smile back at her smugly and silently mouth to her the word "covered".

Her eyes widen. "YOU! You did this to me! I should have known! Officers, arrest her! She set my ass on fire! I'll kill you!"

One officer looks to the other, shaking his head as if to say, "Why didn't I call in sick today?"

The group of them begin walking towards the front door as Majenta continues her rant.

"Why aren't you people doing anything? She's the one who set me on fire! Arrest her! ARREST HER!"

Still wickedly smiling at her, I wait until our closest point before I tell her aloud, "Prove it."

It takes both officers to reign her in, but once Majenta's shouts are muffled by the squad car doors sealing her shut inside, I know the worst is over. I wave them off with a cocktail napkin.

A sudden wave of people push past me towards the bar for their free drinks. I look over and see that Casta Spella is in stitches. She walks over and says, "Ding dong, the wicked bitch is finally dead! Good riddance."

High fiving her, I say, "Ain't that the truth Ruth."

Soon the thumping club music resumes and everyone in the club is holding a fresh cocktail. A good time is eventually had by all.

Just before closing I feel someone tap me on the shoulder.

"Happy New Year Divina."

I turn around and see Mark the sparkler guy standing at my side again. The look in his eyes tells me that he has something more in mind than just a sweet goodbye.

"Derek the bartender invited me over to his place for a nightcap. When I asked if I could invite you over too he seemed really happy that I asked. What do you say? Think you'd care to finish off ringing in the New Year with the both of us?"

Well, well, well. This night just keeps getting better and better.

"What the hell. It's a new year. Maybe I can bend a rule or two just this once."

Fin.

FEBRUARY

VALENTINE'S DAY:
"THE RELUCTANT VALENTINE"
BY WARNER DAVIDSON

WILL U BE MINE?

It was written there in dark blue ink—this time on pink card stock—in that same tidy script as all the others. A big, red heart, cut from construction paper and outlined in silver glitter, adorned the face of the handmade card that had arrived in yesterday's mail. I had intentionally avoided opening it until just this morning, already anticipating what I'd find within. Just like the dozen or so similar cards I'd receive over the last year—on holidays and other auspicious occasions—this card was unsigned.

I turned the envelope over in my hands. Like the others, it was addressed to me—*Robert D. Bakker* (with both k's intact)—in the same fluid, yet masculine cursive hand that had penned the singular question inside of the card the envelope had carried to my door: *Will U B Mine?*

As usual, there was no return address, but the postmark indicated the card had been mailed locally—zip code 20036—my own neighborhood for the past 8 years. A generic, self-adhesive "forever stamp" was affixed to the upper right corner of the plain, white envelope—no chance, then, for a DNA sample. As if I'd even know how to go about testing for such a thing.

Why had I even bothered to open it? I asked myself that same question each time one of these mysterious cards showed up in my mailbox. This had to be someone's idea of a joke—and, as always, I was the punch line.

There was no way, of course, that I actually had a secret admirer—some known or unknown individual, lovesick and lurking, who knew not only the spelling of my uncommon last name, but also my unpublished home address, the date of my birth, and even the exact date that I passed my final CPA exam. Each of those occasions had been marked with a similar handmade card from my invisible friend.

Of course it wasn't a secret admirer, I kept telling myself. How could I even think such a thing? Guys like Robert D. Bakker don't have secret admirers.

It's not that I'm bad looking—in fact, most of the guys I've hooked up with since moving to the District of Columbia have assured me that I've held up quite well for a fella at the ripe, old age of 35. I have a decent enough face, I guess—at least it doesn't send men shrieking at my approach. I work hard to keep my body in shape. I never leave the house unclean or poorly-groomed. I'm very gainfully employed. And, if you'll pardon my bluntness, I'm hung like a circus pony.

So, why not me? With all that I seemingly have going for me, how come I'm still single? Why am I not good enough to be some guy's Mr. Right, while all too often relegated to Mr. Right Now?

Well, for one thing, I have a very bad habit of falling for men who are so far outside of my own league that it would take an ocean liner to close the gap between us. With such ill-fated tastes, it turns out, even money, respectable looks, and an enormous cock aren't enough to assure that love will blossom. The boys who are interested? Well … most of them are in it just for the sex. Let's face it, there's a size queen on every corner in this crazy town, but all they want is a good poke. They're never looking to settle down. No, not these boys! Not with me anyway. Because here, everyone's itching to have that one thing I can't offer them—excitement.

Hello! I'm an accountant! You can't get less exciting than that.

And if there really was a guy out there who had a thing for me—an actual emotional connection that had nothing whatsoever to do with the size of my dick—wouldn't he have at least registered a little bit on my radar? I haven't seen so much as a blip in over a year. In fact, my love life has become so stagnant that if you listen closely you can actually hear crickets chirping.

Getting laid? Well, that I'm able to manage with regular frequency. I like sex and all—quite a bit as the case might be—but, increasingly, casual sex is cold comfort when you crave something much deeper.

So … if it's not a secret admirer, who *is* sending me these cards, and the warm, fuzzy messages scrawled within them in such infuriating, near-perfect penmanship? And really, what kind of guy makes all-occasion greeting cards by hand when there's a CVS Pharmacy on practically every corner?

When the first one arrived—the 15th of last March on my 35th birthday— my immediate thought was that it must have been sent by my crazy Uncle Claude. Old people do sentimental things like that, don't they? Send homemade cards and shit? He's in a nursing home, after all, where they use arts and crafts as therapy to keep the old-timers' minds alert. Perhaps

Claude makes greeting cards. Now, he's certainly dotty enough to send a card without signing it—one maybe … 2 tops … but to send over 30 cards unsigned? Even Uncle Claude's not that loopy. The note in that first card read simply, "Celebrating 35 years of you!" Anyone might have written such a thing. This time, however, it's a Valentine's Day card—a romantic first for my mysterious devotee. It just couldn't be Uncle Claude, right? I think it goes without saying that I found the very notion of my mother's 75-year-old brother sending me a valentine particularly unsettling. I crossed his name off my list of possible suspects.

Perhaps it was a neighbor from my building. After all, I do live in a high-rise condominium with a considerable quotient of gay residents. Who's to say it couldn't be any one of them. I certainly hope it's not that strange, nerdy little fellow down the hall—the one with the skin condition who always lets his dog poop in the flowerbeds. Truth told, the way he looks at me sometimes makes me feel like I need a shower. I'd best keep an eye on that one.

Could it possibly be that hot blonde number from the 8th floor who wears skin-tight t-shirts and too much *Obsession*? Now that's a laugh! He won't even say hello to me in the elevator. Though I could have sworn that one time he actually growled at me.

Grrrr!

I couldn't tell if it was a greeting or simply an attack of gas. No, count him out too.

It's also possible that these cards are the work of one of my friends—some sort of twisted act of compassion. In that case, it would have to be one of my coupled friends—my *smugly* joined-at-the-hip, madly-in-love friends who, no doubt, feel sorry for dear, old, single Rob. Because, after all, another year has come and gone and dear, old, single Rob is still … well … quite wretchedly single. You think I'm joking. I'm not joking. I've actually seen them lean in close to one another at parties and whisper, "He's still single, you know. The poor dear."

SHHHH! If we whisper, maybe he won't realize how pathetic he really is!

Yeah, that's probably the answer to this mystery. My friends are just trying to add a little warmth to my otherwise cold and lonely existence.

Well, whoever this surreptitious card-maker is, he didn't appear to be in any hurry to let me in on his secret ... and the uncertainty was driving me freaking crazy.

So fuck him then!

I dropped the card on the window ledge, on top of the stack of other cards and notes I'd gotten from my anonymous pen pal over the last year. Then I downed the last of my coffee, grabbed my satchel, and headed for work.

* * *

All day at the office I tried valiantly to concentrate on balance sheets, income statements, and amortization tables but my mind kept coming back to that cryptic valentine sitting on my window ledge. I couldn't help but wonder again about the nameless man who had sent it.

Will U B Mine?

What the fuck!

Whoever he was, this guy was really beginning to piss me off. How dare he do such a thing? On Valentine's Day, no less! My whole life I've never been particularly keen on holidays—even more so now since I moved away from my family and spend most holidays alone. On those rare occasions I agree to celebrate holidays with friends, it seems I'm always *the single guy* in room full of couples. No thanks! So, yeah, I'm not what you'd call a lover of holidays, but as they go, Valentine's Day has got to be just about the worst of the lot.

Why? Here's the thing. We're sold this bill of goods that Valentine's Day is the one special day of the year that we honor and celebrate *true love*—in all its glory—with our one and only beloved.

What a pile of horse shit!

I don't have a one and only beloved, and from the looks of things, I probably never will.

As far as I'm concerned, Valentine's Day has nothing at all to do with love—true or otherwise. Everyone knows this holiday was thought up by greeting card companies as an excuse to pick the pockets of sentimental fools on an otherwise unremarkable day in the deadest part of winter.

And what about poor, miserable schmucks like me who do not have a "certain someone special" in our lives? Valentine's Day just ensures that we are reminded at least once each year of just how alone and unlovable we really are.

Why don't they just kick us in the nuts and get it over with?

I'm not asking anyone to feel sorry for me. Most days I'd rather be alone … but Valentine's Day has this devious way of pushing all of my *nobody-loves-me* buttons. So, in lieu of sitting home alone and feeling sorry for myself every February 14th, it has long been my practice to spend this most despicable of days with my best friend—and occasional fuck buddy—Cameron Cole, doing what two unattached gay boys do best to make one another forget their blues. Like me, Cam has never had a problem giving his milk away for free, but as we've both come to realize over the years, getting the boys to buy the cow is an uphill battle. Cam and I have always had each other's backs and, in a pinch, I've always been able to count on him to fill the boyfriend void whenever it's in need of filling—literally as well as figuratively.

Until now, that is. This Valentine's Day, Cam has an *actual* boyfriend—a *steady* guy with all the usual bells and whistles and true love trappings—and for the first time since I met him, he's off limits. Cam met Patrick just before Thanksgiving when he joined the gay bowling league. Go figure! A *bowling* league? Cam doesn't even like to bowl. But desperate is as desperate does, and now he's happy and content and wearing rented shoes two nights each week. I shudder at the thought.

So now I have to face facts. The world as I know it has changed. Cam and Patrick have found each other. They are "in love," or so they assure me at every turn. They call each other cutesy pie names like "Pooky" and "Honey Bear" and no doubt they've already picked out a china pattern for their imminent cohabitation. They're so fucking cute together I could puke.

So … I guess this year it's going to be just me, a few of Titan Media's finest, and a very large tub of Boy Butter. I might as well throw myself into the Pit of Despair right now.

No way. Not this time. I just can't let that happen again. It was time for me to put Plan B in action.

This year, Valentine's Day falls on a Thursday. Under normal circumstances, Thursday nights aren't really what you would call a going-out-on-the-town kind of night for me. In fact, I tend to think of Thursdays as my rest-up-for-Friday night—I usually stay in, order up a pizza or pick up some Chinese takeout on the corner, watch one or several angst-ridden teen dramas on The CW network, suck down a cold one—or two—and get my ass to bed early. But given the likelihood of another Valentine's Day spiral into the abyss, I figured that if I didn't do something to distract myself, I'd be one sorry mess come morning. So, I opted for Plan B—go out and see what kind of trouble I could get into *all by my lonesome*. Surely, I can't be the only single male of the homosexual species out on the prowl this Valentine's Day. Perhaps, if I'm lucky, I'd find a suitably gifted hottie to serve in Cam's stead. A tall challenge if there ever was one.

But where to go? What to do?

Well? What do I always do when I want to pick up a hot stranger for hot stranger sex?

I go to The Bone Zone.

* * *

When I arrived at The Bone Zone, happy hour was still going strong with its usual offering of $2 drafts and two-for-one cocktails. The bar wasn't crowded enough for the kind of hyper-drive cruising that's possible on weekends, but from what I could tell when my eyes finally adapted to the darkness inside, the pickings this evening were surprisingly favorable.

But first things first, I needed some liquid courage.

I made my way to the end of the bar and took my usual seat at J.D.'s station. J.D. Prentice—J.D. being shorthand for Jackson Drew—was, by anyone's standards, the very definition of hotness. This evening, he was totally on fire. Six-feet-four inches of solid muscle, a rugged, masculine face, a square jaw, coarse dark hair cropped short like his perfectly groomed goatee, steel blue eyes, and a smile that could make you cream in your jeans. J.D. was a recent transplant from Houston, and the second best reason to frequent The Bone Zone. What I wouldn't give for just one night alone with him.

Yeah, right. Fat chance.

When he noticed me sitting at the bar J.D. nodded "hello" and smiled broadly, showing off a set of perfect, white teeth.

He walked over ... no, scratch that ... he glided over like a sleek panther stalking its prey ... and stopped directly in front of me.

"Well hey there, handsome, long time no see. What can I get for you?"

His deep Texas drawl made my knees weak.

"Hi J.D. The usual is fine."

"Olives or a twist."

"Olives ... jumbos if you've got 'em."

"I've got a couple a jumbos for you right here." J.D. grinned seductively as he cupped his balls through his skin-tight jeans.

I laughed, all the while imagining what his particular variety of jumbos would feel like slapping against my chin.

"Any particular brand of gin?"

"Make it a Hendrick's. I'm pampering myself tonight."

"Hendrick's it is, coming right up."

I watched as J.D. scooped ice into the shaker and then poured the gin directly from the bottle, ever confident in his pouring skills. He snapped the top tightly on the shaker without adding any Vermouth. J.D., of course, was the only bartender at The Bone Zone who always remembered I like my martinis very dry—yet another reason I never went to any of the other bartenders' stations, no matter how busy the bar was.

As covertly as possible, I sat back on my barstool and admired J.D.'s bulging pecs and biceps while he shook the silver container and then emptied the icy liquid into a chilled martini glass. Right to the rim—a perfect pour, as always. Damn, he was good.

J.D. placed a napkin on the bar in front of me and set the glass on top of it. Then, very gently, he slid the drink close to me.

"Take a sip," he commanded. "We need to make some room for those olives."

Without picking up the glass, I leaned forward and sipped the ice-cold martini, feeling J.D.'s eyes burning into me the whole time.

"Drink a little more."

I took another sip.

Mmmm!

"Perfect," I said, sitting up straight again as J.D speared three jumbo olives with a swizzle stick.

Furtively, J.D. quickly scanned the bar to locate Drake Amidon, The Bone Zone's owner. Satisfied that Drake was preoccupied with another customer, J.D. popped a fourth olive into his mouth.

"Don't tell Drake," he said laughing. "The cheap motherfucker will take it out of my share of tonight's tips."

J.D. slid the skewered olives gently into my glass, its contents once more up to the rim.

I took another sip.

"I was hoping you'd come in tonight, Robbie. I haven't seen you in quite awhile. I was beginning to think you found a new hangout. Or worse. A boyfriend."

"J.D., you know I've only got eyes for you." I kidded, though, truth told, when I was around J.D., it was hard to look at anyone else.

"Just say the word, Robbie boy, and I'm all yours." He winked.

I reached into the back pocket of my jeans and removed my wallet. I took my Visa out of its slot and slid it across the bar toward J.D. "What do I owe you?"

"How about another smile?" He pushed my card back toward me.

"Put your card away, Robbie. Tonight's on me."

I smiled back … my face suddenly very hot.

"Thanks, J.D. I owe you one."

"The pleasure is mine, Robbie."

I slid my Visa back into its slot and slipped him a twenty instead. "At least let me give you a tip."

J.D. palmed the bill without looking at it, and clutched it to his heart. "Thank you," he mouthed silently. His smile was warm and sincere. Then he deposited the bill into the glass tip jar behind the bar.

He turned back to me. "Where's Cam tonight? I'd have thought tonight would be the perfect night for you two young bucks to be out carousing? It is Valentine's Day after all, and here you are out and about without your wing man."

"Haven't you heard?"

"Heard what?"

"Cam's an old, married woman now. His carousing days are over. At least for the time being?"

"You know, come to think of it, just last week one of my other regulars said that Cam had a steady beau now but I just assumed he had his facts confused. I can't picture Cam settling down … with anyone."

"You and me both, but there you have it."

"Wow! If you say so then it must be true. Cam has gotten himself hitched. That's incredible."

"Astounding is the word for it."

Once again, J.D. flashed me his most enticing smile. "Well … then I guess that means there's still hope for you and me."

* * *

I sat on that barstool most of the evening, chatting with J.D and surveying the room from time to time to check out the action, hoping to make a new friend for some horizontal game play later on. Just after 9:00 p.m. I spotted a nice-looking blond with a hot body leaning on the bar rail across the room. He spotted me too. Our eyes locked.

Blondie nodded and raised his glass to me in salute.

Gotcha! Now reel him in … slowly.

I smiled and mimicked his salute. Blondie licked his lip as he let his hand fall slowly to his side, gently brushing his crotch on the way down.

Subtle!

I was just about to get up from my barstool and walk over to him when an even hotter guy, also blonde, joined him at the rail. They kissed, with some rather serious tongue action. The second blonde glared at me as he clutched the ass of the first in both hands. He couldn't have marked his territory any clearer if he'd pissed on the guy.

Damn! So much for that love connection!

I turned back toward the bar. J.D. was standing right in front of me on the other side of the bar, staring at me and grinning as he towel dried a freshly washed beer mug.

"What? You win some, you lose some."

He chuckled. "What are you looking for tonight, Robbie? Maybe I can help you out."

"Not sure exactly. But I'll know it when I see it."

"Tell you what," J.D. responded, "… the bar is slow tonight. They really don't need three bartenders on duty for a crowd this small and, besides, I've been working way too many hours lately and could use a break. I asked Drake if I could leave early tonight and he said yes. I was hoping that maybe you'd like to come home with me."

I chuckled. "Sure, J.D., we could have ourselves a real pajama party … bake cookies and paint each other's toenails. You better be careful saying stuff like that to me. If I thought you really meant it, I'd already be dragging your ass toward the door."

J.D. scowled. He dropped the clean mug he had just finished drying back into the soapy water in the bar sink. Then he put both hands, palm down, on the surface of the bar. He squared his shoulders as he leaned in toward me.

"Why wouldn't you think I meant it, Robbie? I've been hitting on you since I started working here last spring. I comp so many drinks for you that Drake keeps threatening to dock my pay. I see you in here week after week, leaving with a different guy each time. But I practically throw myself at you and turn it into a joke. What's a guy got to do to get your attention?"

I choked on my martini.

"Aren't you even the least bit attracted to me?" he added.

"Of course … I'm attracted," I stammered, stunned by his words. "Quite, in fact! You're the hottest guy in this place. Hell, you're the hottest guy I've ever met."

"Then what's the deal? I've been hitting on you, *hard*, for months … and nothing."

"I thought you were … just joking."

"Why would you think that?"

"Well … you're a bartender … a lot of bartenders flirt with their customers. It's good for tips."

"Yeah … well … you've got a point there, but have you ever seen me coming on to any of the other regulars as relentlessly as I do with you?"

"Well … no, I haven't … now that you ask."

"Any strangers passing through?"

"No."

"Then what gives? We're both single. You've told me many times that you're tired of bed surfing and want to find someone special. You admit that you're attracted to me, and I think I've made it very clear that I'm really into you. So what's the problem here? Do I have bad breath or B.O.? Do you have a strict policy against dating bartenders? I really like you, Robbie, and it hurts my feelings when I ask you out and you make a joke about it. It's Valentine's Day, for Christ's sake, and I just thought that … if you would just give me a chance …."

"I'm sorry, J.D. … I never meant … it's just that … I … I never thought …"

"You never thought what?"

I sighed heavily and looked down at my hands.

"I never thought that a hot guy like you would want to be with a loser like me."

J.D. came around the end of the bar. He walked up behind me and put his arms around my chest. He kissed the top of my head.

"You're no loser, Robbie. You're definitely no loser."

He spun the barstool around so that I was facing him. He reached out and placed his right hand on the back on my neck, drawing me gently to his lips. All I can say is that it was a good thing I was seated because the sensation of his warm tongue melting against my own made my whole body weak, and I collapsed against his chest. With his left arm he held me tight. I could feel the warmth of his skin against my cheek through his t-shirt, and as his fingers stroked my hair I was suddenly flooded with a sense of absolute bliss.

Drake shouted from the other end of the bar. "Prentice … I thought you were leaving. Take that shit somewhere else. This is a place of business, not the back seat of your car."

"I'm going Drake. I've already cleaned my station. Sorry, but I'm taking Robbie with me."

"He's one of my best customers so be sure to hose him down and bring him back when you're done with him."

"Gotcha!" J.D. turned his attention back to me. "My place?"

"Where do you live?"

"In the West End."

"Then let's go to my place. It's closer."

We practically sprinted to the exit.

* * *

Let's just say that if I ever doubted the existence of God, I am now a true believer. Sex with J.D. Prentice is the closest to Heaven a mortal man can come without bursting into a flaming ball of light.

I must have dozed off for a moment afterward, because when I woke again, J.D. was lying on his back beside me. I was on his left, my head resting on his chest. I could hear his steady heartbeat, much slower now than it had been earlier. J.D.'s left arm cradled my shoulder; with his right hand he stroked my forearm lightly, sending chills coursing through my body.

I looked up and he smiled down at me.

"That was really wonderful, Robbie." He kissed my forehead. "I always knew we'd be good together. And my fragile ego truly appreciated your enthusiasm!"

I blushed. "Yeah, I did get a little loud, didn't I?"

He kissed me again, this time on the mouth, and pulled me closer. It felt warm and comfortable—and *safe*—in his arms. I wanted this moment to go on forever. I could scarcely believe that J.D. Prentice was here … in my bed … with *me*! He hadn't rushed out the door as soon as he'd gotten what he came for.

"It really was good, wasn't it?" I agreed. "There was a moment there when I thought I might actually pass out. I'm amazed by your stamina. And where do you hide that thing when you're not using it?"

"What can I say? I'm a grower."

"I'll say you are."

"So … Robbie … are you up for round two?"

"I thought you'd never ask!"

"This time, though, you're on top!"

* * *

An hour later we were still curled up together in my bed, alternately snuggling, kissing, caressing, and dozing. I could hear J.D. breathing softly now beside me as the sky got brighter through my bedroom window.

J.D. had spent the entire night. I couldn't remember the last time a guy had stayed until morning.

He stirred then, and wrapped his arms around me even tighter. When I looked up at his face, his eyes were open and he was smiling.

"Morning handsome." He tussled my hair. "I could get used to this in a real hurry. I've wanted to be with you for so long I can't believe it's finally happening."

"Me too," I admitted openly. "I'm just sorry I didn't catch on sooner. I can be a bit thick sometimes."

"In more ways than one," he added laughing.

I nudged him with my shoulder.

"Are you hungry? I could make us something for breakfast. Eggs and bacon, maybe?"

At the mention of food, J.D.'s stomach growled.

"You don't have to answer that," I said, "your empty belly answered for you."

We got out of bed. I threw on a pair of gym shorts and a t-shirt and then I got a pair of sweatpants and another tee out of my dresser for J.D., both were more than a tad small on him but he didn't seem to mind. We padded, barefoot, out into the kitchen.

I turned on the coffee pot, which I'd set up before going to The Bone Zone, and then I went to the refrigerator and got out everything we would need for breakfast. I asked J.D. if he would set places for us at the kitchen table and told him where everything was.

When the coffee was ready, J.D. poured a cup for both of us and handed me one while I prepared breakfast at the stove. He stepped up behind me and kissed the back of my neck.

"Why don't you take a seat at the table and enjoy your coffee while I finish up here."

J.D. sat down at the table and gazed out the kitchen window.

"It looks like it's going to be a beautiful day today. I really wish you didn't have to work today. Friday is my regular day off. It sure would be great if we could spend the whole day together."

"I could always call in and request a personal holiday. They owe me one."

"You'd do that for me?"

I smiled and nodded.

J.D. looked out the window again.

"What are these?" he asked, indicating the stack of cards sitting on the window ledge.

"Just a bunch of cards."

"What kind of cards?"

"Birthday, holidays, special occasion cards.

"Who are they from?"

"That's just it, I don't know."

"What do you mean you don't know?"

"They all came unsigned."

"You must have *some* idea who sent them?"

"Not a clue."

"C'mon. Not even a guess?"

"Yeah. I have a guess. I'm pretty sure it's just some jackass toying with me."

"Some jackass, huh?"

"Who else would send me anonymous cards and notes for nearly a year without revealing his identity? I think, whoever he is, he's just trying to mess with my head."

"That's a pretty negative way to look at it, don't you think? I think you're being too hard on yourself." He picked up the stack of cards and shuffled through them. "To be honest, I think these cards are kind of sweet. Maybe it's someone who really likes you but was hoping for you to make the first move."

"I'd have to know who he was to make a move on him, wouldn't I?"

"People don't always notice what's right in front of them."

"You've got a good point, but guys like me don't have secret admirers."

"So says the man who thought I was joking all those times I asked him out!"

"Touché!"

We both laughed.

J.D. took another sip of his coffee.

"Robbie?"

When I turned toward him, he was standing next to the table with a huge grin on his face.

"Yeah?"

"I'm really *not* a jackass."

"Of course, you're not a …!"

Like I said, I can be a little thick sometimes, so it took a moment to register what he'd just said. When I finally realized what he was telling me, my insides practically melted.

"You sent them?" I whispered as tears of happiness welled up in my eyes.

"I did."

In an instant, I was across the room and in his arms. We kissed deeply, and then he held me, pressing my head against his chest.

"So *will* you?" he asked softly.

"Will I what?"

"Will you be mine?"

I hesitated for only a second.

"Yes, J.D. I'd like that … I'd like that very much."

ACADEMY AWARDS®:
"I'D LIKE TO THANK THE ACADEMY"
BY ROBBIE TURSI-MASICK

"What do you mean you're bringing someone?!" I huffed into the receiver.

"What part didn't you understand?" Jessica said back, "I'm bringing someone to your big, gay Oscar party. What's the big drama?"

"The big drama is that I only invite people that I know and I don't know if I'll have enough food!"

"Yeah, you invite the same people every year and I'm the only one who actually shows up," she said back. "Also, you make enough food to feed the entire West Coast so cut the shit."

"Shut up, I like to be prepared," I said. "Who is this person anyway?"

"Well, ok, you remember that nerdy guy I always talk about that works with me?" she said excitedly.

"No."

"Yes, you do! He's one of the IT guys that frequents my cubicle," she said.

"You have an IT person at your cubicle every day, Jess, because you don't even know how to turn your monitor on," I said as I checked the mini-quiches in the oven. I do tend to go overboard whenever I have a party, but at least I will have food for the week.

"Not the point, you turd," Miss Thing was getting hostile now. "He's a big movie nerd and has had a countdown calendar to the Oscars on his desk for the past couple of months."

"Why the hell were you at his desk?" I questioned. "Oh God, tell me you're sleeping with him. This isn't another asshole I'm going to have hear about dumping you in a week, is he?" Jessica has had worse (or better) luck in men that I ever have. She goes on a date and within a week, she puts out on the third date and then the guy mysteriously disappears. "You work with him, Jess, you can't be doing that shit."

She laughed, "I never said I was sleeping with him! Nor do I think I ever will. He's not really my type." As long as it had a penis, it was Jessica's type. "Come on," she whined, "he's a good guy. You'll like him."

"Whatever," I said, giving up. "But, you better not make out on my couch, I just steam cleaned it."

She laughed again loudly. "No worries, I promise. We'll be there before the red carpet show," she said and then hung up.

Fuck, I almost forgot about that. Jess and I love to watch the celebrities walk down the infamous red carpet and be interviewed by that bitch who has everything, Ryan Seacrest. Jessica loves to comment on the beautiful and downright hideous dresses while I sit and wonder why I don't have Ryan's job. I can dip myself into orange marmalade, making my skin look like a leather couch from the 70s and get into an Armani suit to interview people with twenty times more talent than I'll ever have, too, you know.

I think my "normal" looks will get in the way though.

It was 5:45 so I only had a little time to get myself and my apartment ready. When Jessica says she's going to be somewhere on time, that usually means about twenty minutes early to the rest of the world. Since the red carpet extravaganza starts at 7, I had less than an hour to get my shit together. I quickly took a shower and didn't bother to shave because #1, I hate shaving and #2, Jessica and her new sex toy are coming so I didn't have to impress anyone. I got dressed in a worn out Buffy the Vampire Slayer t-shirt and a pair of baggy jeans I found in a pile of clothes.

As I started to put various chips and dips in serving, the annual text message apologies started to make my phone go ape shit.

"Sry. Can't come 2nite. Next yr!"

"I have to walk my dog."

"OMG! Ur party is today?!?!?! Fuuuck! I'm in Maui."

I need better friends.

After I sent my usual, "It's OK. TTYL" reply texts, I put half the plates and silverware I took out back into my kitchen cabinets. Guess I'm going to be eating mini-quiches and Doritos for the next month. I just sat down and turned on E!, when the door bell rang.

6:40. Right on time, Jessica.

"Coming," I called out and went to the door. I opened it and saw Jessica standing there with a bottle of cheap vodka in one hand and bag of pretzels in the other. We're a classy bunch. "Hello, dear," I said as I gave her a peck on the cheek and took the bottle out of her hand. "Ooh, $10.99, you splurged this time," I said dryly.

She slapped me on the shoulder, "Like you give a shit. Now get out of my way, I'm starving." She pushed me out of the way and made a beeline to the chip bowl.

I stuck my head out the door and looked up and down the hallway. "Umm, Jess? Where's your date?"

She stopped stuffing her face for two seconds to say, "Parking his car," and moved on to the bean dip. Guess she really wasn't planning on making out with anyone tonight. Or in the next three days.

I closed the door behind me and went to the kitchen to open the bottle of vodka. "Haven't eaten this week again?" I said to Jessica and indicated she had melted cheese hanging from the corner of her mouth.

She shook her head, "Not really. It was either get Wendy's or pay my phone bill." Jessica was thin enough as it is, but her eating habits took a back seat to her social life.

I wish I was that lucky.

I went to get some cranberry juice when there was a knock at the door. "Jess, can you get that?" I asked as I dug my way to the back of the refrigerator.

"No prob," she answered while licking her fingers clean.

I heard the door open and Jessica say, "Come on in!" and then deeper voice say, "Thanks. Parking was a nightmare."

It really is by my building. Hopefully his car is in my neighborhood. I closed the fridge door and turned around to meet Mr. Nerdalicious and almost dropped the jar of juice all over my kitchen floor.

Now, when you normally hear that someone's a geek or nerd, your brain automatically thinks of the ones in movies with tape holding their bottle glasses together, pants hitched up to their pits and snot slowly making its way out of their right nostril.

The "nerd" in front of me was something entirely different. Sure, he did have the glasses but there wasn't a trace of masking tape to be found. He was wearing a baggy, zipped up hoodie along with straight cut jeans and black boots. His brown hair was shaggy and wavy, but not messy, and curled up at the ends. Think of Sam Winchester in the first season of Supernatural.

Yes, that's where my mind goes. I describe people's looks by their similarity to fictional characters.

I, myself, look like an older version of Glee's Kurt Hummel minus the fabulous hair, fashion sense and ability to sing.

Oh, and Jessica? Well, she looks just like any dormitory slut that dies within the first ten minutes of a horror movie so use your imaginations.

"Josh, this is my best friend in the entire universe, Nick," Jess said, while motioning to me to come over. "Nick, this is Josh," and she patted him on the shoulder. He stood there awkwardly with his hands in his pockets and smiled sheepishly.

I broke out of my daze and walked over to him. "Nice to meet you, Josh," I said and stuck out my right hand to shake his. He cocked his head to the side and looked down at my hand which was still holding the cranberry juice. "Oh," I laughed and put the bottle on the counter. "Take two," I joked with a red face and this time he shook my empty hand lightly.

"You as well," he said and quickly returned his hand into his pocket like I just gave him herpes.

"Please sit and make yourself at home," I said to him. "Would you like a drink? Jess and I are usually half in the bag by the time they get to the interpretive dance number. It's the only way we can make sense of it." And really, how else can you make sense of people pirouetting to the score of The Hurt Locker?

"No thanks," he said quietly. "I'll just have a water if that's cool."

Looks: 10, Fun: 3. Oh, well. At least Jess will enjoy him in the sack as long as it doesn't involve conversation.

"I'll get it, Nicky," Jess said and she grabbed a bottle of water from the fridge as well as the tray of quiches from the counter. "Here ya go, Josh," and she handed him the water and shove the tray in his face. "You should try some of these. Nick makes them all homemade. No frozen aisle crap." She nodded her head eagerly.

"Thank you," Josh said and he grabbed one stuffed with cheese. He took a few bites as Jess and I watched his reaction. He looked at us both strangely and said, "Very good." The two of us sighed at the same time then looked at each other and started laughing. Josh just sat there, quietly judging us I'm sure.

He started to scope out my living room taking in the various pictures and large bookcase stuffed with books, DVDs and a few CDs. His eyes squinted a bit and I assumed he was trying to make out the titles of various movies I had. I silently prayed he didn't see Catwoman. (It was on sale, leave me alone.) "Excited for the awards?" I asked him but it didn't stop his analyzation.

"Yeah," he grunted while his face went from amused to disgusted to intrigued to neutral as he scanned the bookshelves.

I looked at Jess with a "What the fuck did you bring to my house?" look and she just shrugged.

"So...I hear you're quite the movie buff," I said to Josh before his eyes reached the Lindsay Lohan section of my DVDs. "Jess says you know pretty much everything there is to know about them."

"Huh?" he said as looked in my direction. "Oh, yeah, I guess." He looked down at his interlocked fingers as his face turned a slight shade of red. He certainly was adorable. "It's just a hobby, really."

"Bullshit!" Jessica yelled, startling both Josh and me. "He has a blog and everything," she said to me with a wink. Josh looked mortified.

"Come on, Josh. You're like the Rainman of Oscars," she said to him with a little tap on his shoulder.

He brushed the bangs out of his eyes as his face turned to crimson. "N-no, I'm not," he muttered softly.

"Oh, yeah?" Jess said. "Who won best supporting actress in...let's see...1954?"

He looked from Jess to me and back again before finally sighing. "Eva Marie Saint for 'On The Waterfront,'" he said positively, "but everyone knows that because Marlo Brando won for best actor and it won for best film." He took a gulp of air. "Right?"

Jess and I cocked our heads, Scooby-style and Josh went back to analyzing his fingernails.

"Ooh!" Jess screeched. "The red carpet arrivals are starting!" She grabbed the remote and turned up the volume. "Uck, why does Ryan Seacrest exist?"

"To pollute our lives with fat-assed rich bitches and keep self-tanning companies in business," I responded. Jess laughed but Josh looked confused.

"What?" I asked him.

"I don't get it," he said, "Who's Ryan Seacrest?"

"Seriously?" Jess and I said simultaneously.

"Yeah, I don't know who he is," he said.

"You're lucky," I said. "He works for E! and produces really, really bad reality shows."

Josh just shrugged.

"He hosts American Idol?" I said. What planet is this kid from?

"Oh, that's that singing show, right?" he said, somewhat relieved.

"Yes, if you can call it that half the time," I answered.

"My ex used to watch it," Josh said like he just ate a lemon. "I hate most TV but he was addicted to that shit."

Something started to swell in my throat and I barely got out the word, "He?"

"Yes," Josh said, looking at me strangely. "Did you think I was straight or something?"

"I...umm..." I stuttered and looked over to Jessica for help. She just sat there with a shit-eating grin on her face.

That bitch. No wonder why she said Josh wasn't her type! He's gay and cute and OH SHIT WHAT IS SHE TRYING TO DO TO ME?!

"Uh, Jess?" I said with a plastered smile. "Can I talk to you for a minute?"

"Sure!" she said with the same kind of smile. "What's up, buttercup?"

"In the other room." I gave her a death stare and she got up off the couch with a sigh. "Excuse us one sec, Josh. Just take notes on who Julia Roberts is wearing this year, OK?" I grabbed Jess's arm and dragged her into the bathroom barely hearing Josh say, "What do you mean 'who'?"

I slammed the door as Jess sat down on the closed toilet seat and tried hard not to start laughing her ass off. "Problem?" she said and giggled.

"WHAT ARE YOU DOING?!" I yelled, well, whispered loudly.

"Whatever could you mean?" she asked while playing with the toilet paper roll and smiling like a devil.

"You're trying to set me up with someone without the tiniest bit of warning?!" I said to her.

"Yes!" she whispered back. "If I told you earlier, you would've cancelled the whole party because you would've freaked out!"

"I AM freaking out!" I yelled then quickly covered my mouth. "Is he even aware that he's being set up?"

Jess avoided eye contact when she said, "Umm...sorta?"

"'Sorta'?"

"Well, he was telling me about movies and spending tonight alone so I said I had a friend that was having a party," she admitted. "And that my friend was adorable and very single."

I almost lunged at her throat but closed my eyes and took a deep breath. "First of all, I hate you. Secondly, I look like I just lost the White Trash Beauty Pageant."

"Oh, stop it. You look fine," she said but I didn't believe a word.

My shirt had holes in it and my jeans haven't been washed in days. I think there's some sauce on one of the knees and I can't tell you when the last time I had spaghetti was.

"I have to change," I said and made my way to the door.

"No!" Jess bellowed as she blocked my way. "Will you stop? There's nothing wrong with the way you look! Well, maybe you could've shaved but that's beside the point." I rubbed my face thinking that would get rid of the stubble. "You always worry about the way you look in front of guys to the point that your personality goes down the drain."

"But..." I said and couldn't think of a reasonable argument. She was right. I've worn "fashion forward" clothes and put gallons of gel in my hair and what has it got me besides credit card debt and sticky pillowcases?

"Precisely," she said with a smirk. I growled in response. "Come on. Let's go back out there before his explodes from all the retarded questions Ryan asks celebrities."

"Fine, but let me just change-"

"NO."

I sighed and opened the door. I jumped and screamed like a girl like I just saw a ghost. Josh was standing there with his hand up as if he was about to knock.

"Sorry," he said, trying to suppress his laughter, "didn't mean to scare you. Thought I'd let you know that Julia Roberts was just on and she's wearing Donna Carpenter or someone."

I smiled at his cute attempt to know something as ridiculous as Donna Karen. "Thanks. We're just on our way out. I think the quiches were agreeing with Jess's stomach." I looked back at her and gave her a look that said, "you owe me this much."

She got what I was trying to convey and said, "Ooh, yeah. All that cheese gives me gas." Josh looked revolted. "Nick here was helping me look for some Tums."

He looked at both of us and knew we were lying.

"Let's get back to the show, shall we?" I said, filling in the awkward silence.

Josh nodded and we all went back to the living room. I made a beeline to the recliner but Jess beat me to it which left the loveseat for Josh and me. I could just sit on the floor but it's hard as a rock even with carpeting. He sat down first and moved all the way over to the arm of couch, leaving me plenty of room to sit. I hope my breath didn't smell like ass.

"So," Jess said, "who else did we miss?"

"Uh," Josh grunted, "Brad Pitt, George Clooney and some chick named Miley Cyrus."

"Blech," I said, "I hate her. She became such a whore after she left Nickelodeon and started making 'movies." Jess laughed and Josh just sat there. What the fuck? Usually my Miley jokes make everyone giggle. "What? You like her or something?" I smiled at him.

He raised an eyebrow and said, "Well, she certainly isn't the cinematic genius that Lindsey Lohan is."

Ouch. Insert gut punch here. In my defense, Lindsey Lohan is an idiot but she made some fun movies when she was sober. Ask any gay and I'll bet you he can quote at least one scene from "Mean Girls".

Josh smiled a crooked smile which I didn't know was supposed to be flirty or downright mocking. Either way my face turned red and started to count the cracks in the ceiling.

"Oh! Look!" Jess broke the uncomfortable silence. "It's starting!" She looked at me with an apologetic glance meaning she's sorry that she's trying to hook me up with a snob.

"I think I'm going to get a drink," and I did just that without asking my guests. It didn't seem to matter because Jess was downing the rest of the bottle of vodka she brought and Josh was in a trance watching the opening monologue by Whoopi Goldberg. I poured myself a glass of wine and swallowed it in two gulps, making me instantly tipsy. I refilled the glass then waddled my ass back over to the living room and plopped down on the couch. Josh slightly bounced up but it didn't seem to matter because the Best Editing category was highly more interesting.

"So you're really into this, huh?" I asked him with a slight slur.

Josh grunted which I suppose meant "yes".

"I see," I responded as the show went to a commercial and Jessica burped.

"Can I have some more water?" Josh asked completely unfazed by my demure friend.

"Umm, sure," I said. "You sure you don't want anything harder? I mean this thing is going to be on for another 12 hours so you'll totally sober up by then." I laughed with a hiccup.

Josh raised an eyebrow and said, "No, water is just fine. I don't drink on nights I have to work in the morning. And it's just a little warm in here."

"Shit, I'm sorry about that," I said as I went to the fridge for a bottle of water. "This building is old and the heat can be a little wonky sometimes. I've gotten used to it over the years. You want me to open a window?"

"Nah, it's all right," he said and I heard the unzipping of his hoodie from behind me as I grabbed the water.

I turned around and dropped the bottle, making it bounce then roll across the room.

It seems that Josh wasn't season one Sam Winchester but more like season four when he put on about 30 pounds of rock hard muscle. I'll give you a moment to Wikipedia that shit.

Ok, so now you know what was sitting in front of me.

The mild mannered blogger had the body of a Superman.

I stood there with my hand in midair clinging onto the imaginary bottle of Poland Spring as I gaped at him. He was wearing a white V-neck T-shirt that drew the eyes to the valley in between his pecs. The sleeves looked like they were about to rip if he made the slightest movement making his bicep flex. I felt something stir in the bottom half of my body just at the thought.

I have no idea how long I stood there, quietly constructing different scenarios all in which Josh was wearing nothing more than a loincloth, when Jessica bumped into me as she ran to the bathroom muttering, "I'm gonna puke!" and slamming the door behind her.

"Umm, she ok?" Josh asked as he got up.

"What?" I said, still in a fog. "Oh. Yeah, she'll be fine." I really had no idea but I'm quite positive she was going all Exorcist in my bathroom right about now. I searched the ground and picked up the water bottle. "Sorry I dropped this," I said as I handed it to him. "Slippery little sucker."

He grinned widely. "Pretty Woman," he said.

"Huh?" I said with confused look.

"Pretty Woman," he repeated. "You just quoted it."

My mind was still on a seven second delay when I realized what I said. "You're right. I have the tendency to spout out random movie lines at any given moment of the day. I'm weird like that. Thank God, we're not watching the Tonys because I might just bust out into song."

He laughed. "I'm sure your voice is beautiful," he said and continued laughing.

"Oh, God no," I said. "When I sing in the shower, I'm pretty sure the water can't wait to get down the drain."

He laughed a deep laugh that vibrated even my chest...and other parts.

We stood there looking at each other as we giggled until the laughter subsided and the sound of the bathroom door being opened made us turn to see Jessica standing as sloppy as her hair.

"I think," she hiccupped, "I'm going to go."

"Jess, are you sure?" I said.

"Do you need a ride?" Josh said with a hint of disappointment on his face.

"No, I'm good," she responded. "In between vomiting up my lungs and shoes, I called a cab."

"She has them on speed-dial," I said to Josh quietly and tried to hide my laughter.

"Remind me never to spend less than 10 bucks on a bottle of booze ever again," she said to no one in particular.

Josh and I just nodded.

Jess grabbed her pocketbook and walked to the door. "You two kids be good," she said to us with a wagging finger. "And if you can't be good, be safe." She winked drunkenly and left the apartment but not without tripping on her own feet twice.

Josh and I stared at the door. "She going to be alright?" he asked.

"Yeah," I said. "She's a mess but we wouldn't want her any other way."

"I guess not," Josh said and looked at the television. "Oh, shit. It's back on." He ran back to couch.

I had to laugh.

"What?" he said as he looked up at me.

"Nothing," I said innocently. "It's just that you look like a kid waiting for the Saturday morning cartoons to start." I smiled. "It's cute."

Oh shit. Did I just say that? I quickly covered my mouth like an idiot. Dammit, Jess, why did you have to be a drunken bitch tonight and leave me here alone with a dreamy guy and my stupidity.

His cheeks blushed slightly and averted his eyes back to the screen. Great, now I think I'm a moron.

"So, what's your favorite movie?" I asked trying to recover.

"I don't think you have the time to hear all of them," he said without taking his eyes off the screen.

"Try me," I said and sat next to him.

He swallowed and looked at me. "Well, I separate them into categories like comedy or drama. Then I separate those into subcategories by year."

"I see," I said slightly impressed but really confused.

"Told you that we would be here for awhile," he said with a chuckle.

"Ok, so give me just one and I'll let you know if I agree with you," I smiled at him.

He smiled back, "Fine. Citizen Kane."

"Hmm...never saw it," I said.

He looked like I just stabbed him in his chest. (His beautifully chiseled chest that is. Sorry, drunken horny moment.)

"Seriously, I haven't and pick up your jaw before your saliva stains my couch," I said to him.

"But, it's an American cinema classic!" he said.

"Sorry," I said sheepishly. "I do know the sled was named Rosebud if that's any consolation but that's only because of episode of Animaniacs.

Oh and the guy's house was named Xanadu and I know that because Xanadu is one of my favorite movies."

"Really? One of the worst movies ever made is one of your favorites?" he said.

"Excuse me?!" I said. "How dare you insult Australian's national treasure, Olivia Newton-John!"

He sighed, "Ok, sure. Sorry I insulted a movie that was written by two guys on an acid trip." He rolled his eyes. "How about you? Besides Xanadu, what's another favorite movie of yours?"

"I don't think I want to tell you for fear of you berating me and me forced to kick your ass," I said with venom.

"Go ahead and try," he said with a smirk.

No fair. He can't look at me like that and not expect me to jump on his face.

"Fine. One of my top 3 movies, and I will seriously hurt you if you say anything negative about it, is Clue."

He didn't make a peep.

"Go ahead, say it," I said. "The cinematography sucked or the costumes were boring. Bring it on."

He just sat there and adjusted his glasses, silently judging me, I'm sure.

He then turned to me, grabbed the front of my shirt and said loudly with eyes wide open, "I CAN'T UNLOCK THE DOOR WITHOUT THE KEY!" He smiled evilly, just inches from my face.

I sat there, breathing heavily with his hands still grasping my already worn shirt. "Did you just quote Mr. Green?" I said while I panted.

He nodded and let go of my shirt. Half of me was relieved while the other half mentally kicked myself for not planting one on him when I had the chance.

"What?" he asked. "You think you're the only one who can quote movies?"

I shrugged. "I just figured you being the movie snob you are, you wouldn't like that kind of movie."

"A snob huh? I'm hurt," he grabbed his chest dramatically like he was shot then laughed. "Come on, though. That movie is not only funny but the cast is incredible. Tim Curry, Michael McKeon, Christopher Lloyd, Eileen Brennan, Leslie Ann Warren..."

"Madeline Kahn," we said at the same time.

"My Maddie," I said with some sadness. "You know I cried for almost a week straight when she passed?" I really did. "I remember being in college when one of my friends told me about her losing her battle with Cancer. I know it sounds weird that I would feel that much for someone I never even met but she was and still is one of my idols."

"Understandably so," he said in an even tone. "She was a great talent both in her comedic and dramatic roles. You know she was nominated for an Oscar twice, right?"

"Sure did," I said proudly. "One for Blazing Saddles and the other for Paper Moon."

"I must say I'm impressed," Josh said.

"She also was nominated three times for a Tony but only won one," I said and Josh genuinely surprised. "You may know Oscar but Tony is a good friend of mine."

He laughed. "Well, maybe on our next date, you can fill me in on all your Tony knowledge."

If I had water in my mouth, this is the part where I would've done a spit take. "Next date?" I gurgled.

"Well, we are alone and having a good time, aren't we?" he asked. I nodded. "And I think you're even cuter in person than your picture."

"My picture?" I said. "Jessica. That bitch. I can only imagine which one she showed you."

"Actually she showed me more than one on her Facebook," he confessed. "Specifically the ones from Bermuda."

"Are you serious?" I whined. "I got so sunburned on that trip, I looked like Sebastian the Crab!" I buried my face in a couch pillow.

He laughed and tapped me on the back. "You did not and don't be upset with her and do NOT tell her I told you about the picture. She'll kill me."

"Not if I kill her first," I said through the pillow. I turned my head sideways but still couldn't look at him from embarrassment. "It's bad enough that she didn't give me any warning that she was setting up a blind date for me."

"Oh," he said. "You didn't know?"

I sat up. "Do you really think that I would look like this if I knew she was bringing you with your sexy Winchester hair and biceps that could crush a walnut?"

He looked confused. "Winchester hair? Is that a good thing?"

"It's VERY good thing," I said.

"Oh. OK," he said. "So does that mean you're attracted to me?" He grinned.

I rolled my eyes. "Ya think?"

"Yeah, that whole dropping the water bottle thing when I took off my sweatshirt was really subtle," he said.

"Shut up!" I shrieked and whacked him in the shoulder with the pillow.

"She said to wear this, too," he said while laughing and trying to block my assault.

"OK, now she's really dead," I said. "But you first!" and I hit him again which only brought on more husky laughter.

After the third hit, he grabbed my hand with the pillow in it. "Got ya," he said.

"Oh, do you now?" I said with a smirk.

"Yup," he said and was on top of me in a second.

"Well, this certainly wasn't planned either," I said, trying to control my breath and hormones.

"You may not think so," he said as he blew his bangs out of eyes, "but I've wanted to do this since you answered the door tonight."

I laughed. "Hover above me on my couch?"

"No," he said. "This," and he leaned down to press his lips to mine.

I slowly closed my eyes and let his warm mouth take control. He reached behind me to support my head as I ran my fingers through his soft hair, softly caressing his head. He deepened the kiss and I moaned quietly.

Nerds certainly know how to make out.

"Wait a minute! Wait a minute!" I pushed him off of me slightly. "What about the awards?"

He looked over at the TV then back at me with that devilish smile. "Fuck it," and he kissed me again.

MARCH

ST. PATRICK'S DAY:
"PATRICK TAKES A HOLIDAY"
BY ALAN SMITHEE

Once upon a time there was a leprechaun named Patrick. Patrick lived in the country of Ireland under a large oak tree with his family. Now Patrick wasn't like the other leprechauns. While his comrades learned about gold, rainbows, and magic in school, Patrick could often be found reading fashion magazines under his desk or doodling new clothing lines in his notebook.

"Patrick! Are you drawing dresses again?", his teacher would ask.

"Yes Mrs. O'Hara.", Patrick would often answer back.

Patrick was no stranger to school detention either. In fact, he had a permanent seat reserved for him daily. He really didn't mind though. Detention gave Patrick lots more time to perfect the dress designs he wasn't able to finish in class.

When it was time to go home, Patrick would often race his way back to the family oak tree to catch the latest episode of Project Runway.

"Patrick Derby O'Gillian, are you watching that Project Runway again?", his father would ask. "When are you gonna give up all that nonsense and become a respectable leprechaun like your brothers? You have a proud legacy to carry on you know."

Groaning, Patrick would usually reply, "But dad, I don't WANT to hide gold for the rest of my life and give wishes to slovenly dressed slugs. I want to create the most beautiful couture the world has ever seen!"

Patrick's father would then just shake his head and walk away.

One day while watching reruns of his favorite fashion television show, Patrick's life changed all in the span of a brief commercial. Dazzling supermodel Heidi Klum and silver haired fashionista Tim Gunn looked straight into the camera smiling their brilliant smiles and said the following forever immortalized words:

"Are you looking to become the world's newest fashion designer? Think you have what it takes to make the cut? Auditions to be on the next season of Project Runway are underway. Go to the website shown below and register for your spot at the chance of becoming the next household name in the fashion world."

As if hypnotized into a wonderful trance, Patrick bolted up and made a mad dash towards the family computer. When he got there he found his little sister Mary Catherine looking at the latest online photos of her singing idol Justin Bieber O'Leary. Pushing her aside, Patrick typed in the web address he had just seen on television and watched as the pimply faced tween on the computer screen transformed into the two iconic fashion titans he had just seen before.

"Hey! I was here first! I'm telling mom!"

Ignoring the fervent cries of his bratty little sister, Patrick skimmed through the site until he found what he was looking for. There, printed on the screen in front of him, was the online application form. With shaky hands he typed in the necessary information and hit submit. As soon as he did, a new box appeared with a date, address, and list of required items that would be needed for the audition. Was he reading this right? Auditions were to be held the very next day in New York City? This was too good to be true!

Patrick raced up the knobby stairway towards his room. Grabbing his travel bag from the closet, he stuffed all the essentials into it, noting that he'll probably need a second bag for all his hair products.

Just at that moment Patrick's parents walked in.

"Did you push your sister off the computer chair young man?"

Zipping by them to his closet to look through his latest creations, Patrick tells them, "Not now. I'm packing for my trip to New York City."

Astonished, his parents repeat loudly, "NEW YORK CITY?!"

Grabbing the most colorful dresses available, Patrick takes an empty box in the corner and carefully starts folding the fabulous frocks into it.

"Yeah, I'm going to audition to be on the next season of Project Runway. Auditions are tomorrow. I have SO much to prepare!"

Guffawing, Patrick's father says, "Over my dead body! Tomorrow is St. Patrick's Day. It's the busiest day of the year for our family! Ain't no son of mine skirting his traditional duties to go gallivanting off to some strange city on the other side of the world to show some dresses!"

Continuing to ignore his parents, Patrick remembers the new set of high heels he had created a month ago and retrieves the box from the closet to place them on top of the now packed dresses.

"Saints and begorrah, it's like talking to a brick wall. Did you hear me young man? You are gonna help your brothers and I hide our gold like we have every year and you're gonna like it! You live under MY tree so you're gonna live by MY rules!"

Biting off a piece of packing tape with his teeth, Patrick seals shut the box of dresses and shoes and begins writing the memorized New York address he had just seen on the computer. Snapping his fingers, the box disappears like magic.

Turning back to his parents, Patrick tells them, "I'm 108 years old. I was bound to leave home SOME time. Looks like as good a time as any. You, Brien, Seamus and Finnegan will be just fine without me. I only slow you down anyway."

Fuming with rage, Patrick's father shouts, "FINE! You wanna spit on your family's heritage then you can find a tree of your own to live in! I've had enough of your craziness. No son of mine will ever be a DESIGNER and live under MY roof!"

Storming off, Patrick's father slams the bedroom door behind him for added effect. Seeing the situation for what it is, Patrick's mother takes his hand and says, "He didn't mean it dear. He'll come around. You make lovely dresses Patrick, but...is this really what you want to do with your life?"

Kissing his mother on the cheek, Patrick says, "It's what I am mother. I was born a designer and now it's time for me to live the life of one! I'm gonna be a big name some day. You just wait and see!"

Sitting on his bed, Patrick's mother sighs and says, "Well, if this is what truly makes you happy then I support you son. But you just be careful, you hear? I hear awful stories about designers who go wrong."

Snickering, Patrick replies, "Don't worry about me. I'm gonna be bigger than Halston!"

Smiling at her son, Patrick's mother helps him finish his packing before magically sending them off as well. Just after, a small sack materializes into her hands.

"What's that?" Patrick asks her.

"Oh, this is a little something that I've been socking away for a rainy day. My son is about to leave for a big strange city. It's about as rainy a day as it can get for me."

At that Patrick sees a tear fall from his mother's face. Wiping it away and giving her the biggest hug he can, Patrick says, "I can't take that mother. That gold is for you!"

"Poppycock!", his mother says in response. Straightening out his green suit, she continues, "Consider it an investment. Now you watch yourself while you're out there, you hear?"

Taking his wooden shillelagh from the corner of the room, she hands it to Patrick.

"Now be gone with ye. Sláinte is táinte."

"Health and wealth to you too mother." Patrick replies.

* * *

When Patrick magically re-materializes, he finds himself standing in the middle of New York's Times Square. The bright lights, bustling people and overall energy of the city energizes Patrick's already overjoyed spirit. It seems everywhere he looks he finds some new wonderful curiosity to marvel over.

To his surprise and wonder, Patrick notices a photo shoot is taking place underneath the largest video jumbotron billboard. Walking over to it, he is amazed to see famous supermodel Cindy Crawford in the middle of the flashing lights and growing crowd of tourists surrounding it. When Patrick finishes walking through the forest of tourist legs, he could clearly see the supermodel in all her glory. Only thing was, Cindy did not look at all happy. The expression on her face is sad, which only matched the horrible frock she is wearing in front of the cameras.

The photographer didn't look at all happy either. Upon closer inspection, Patrick recognized the photographer as well. It was former supermodel turned fashion photographer Janice Dickinson. Normally known for her no-nonsense demeanor, she too looked like she sympathized with her well known subject.

"Enough! You two are supposed to be two of the best in the business. So why can't I see any results! I knew I should have gone with Claudia Schiffer and someone who knows how to operate a camera!"

A fury began to boil in Patrick's blood. Who would DARE say such horrible things to two such huge powerhouses of the fashion industry?

That's when he saw her. Standing in the corner pulling her hair out was a prissy dark haired woman who looked as if the scowl on her face was a permanent expression she held in her day-to-day life.

"Everyone take five! Evidently we're not getting anything out of these two at the moment. Hopefully when we get back there will be an improvement."

Huffing off the set, the clothing designer went to her trailer and slammed the door shut. Patrick suddenly felt the urge to wish a bad luck curse on the young upstart. Instead he wandered over to Cindy and Janice, who were deep into a private discussion.

"Who the fook is that witch and WHY is she allowed to yell at ye two that way?"

Normally Patrick is very proper when meeting new people, especially when it comes to fashion celebrities he admires. Too angered to engage in formalities, he jumps right to the point.

Looking down at his 3'8" frame, the two women are taken by surprise.

Continuing, Patrick says, "Cindy, you have worked with some of the most influential artists of all time and have graced the covers of countless magazines. The same can be said of you Janice. Why would either of you let some nobody", Patrick grabs the hem of Cindy's dress, "obviously no talent hack speak to you that way?"

Obviously enamored with Patrick's blunt yet observant comment, Cindy smiles and says, "You do notice a lot, don't you…"

At that, Patrick removes his bowler hat and bows low to the ground.

"My name is Patrick Derby O'Gillian and you are looking at the next future winner of Project Runway. I'm honored to make your acquaintance."

Cindy and Janice look at each other and smile.

"Well, if you must know Patrick", Cindy answers, "I'm letting that fanged tarantula boss me around because this is a charity shoot. All proceeds go to a national leukemia fund that I'm trying to raise money for. Janice is here as a personal favor to me."

"That's right." Janice continues. "And believe me, I wouldn't be here taking this shit if it wasn't for a good cause. I outta kick that monster in the balls."

Feeling for their predicament, Patrick says, "What if I presented you with a proposition that doubled what you are probably getting from that rag designer and helped me out at the same time?"

Unsure but curious, Janice says, "Go on..."

"Well, I normally don't like to brag about such things, but my family is very wealthy. If I were able to help you double the money you were to get from HER", Patrick thumbs toward the trailer behind them, "would you both consider modeling my sample dresses for the Project Runway judges tomorrow? I couldn't think of a better way to get my name noticed than by having such royal members of the fashion world wearing my designs."

Cindy awkwardly says, "I don't mean to insult you Patrick, but the money we're getting for this photo shoot isn't anything to sneeze at. Evil as she may be, that woman is going to write us a check for one million dollars. Can you really guarantee that we'll receive double that amount?"

Smiling broadly, Patrick beams, "Is that all?"

Taking out the bag of gold his mother gave him, Patrick takes out a handful of coins and places them in his pocket. He then hands the rest of the bagged gold coins to the potential clients before him.

"I think you'll find that me bag has well OVER double the money you were looking for."

Wide-eyed, Cindy and Janice seem surprised at what to say next.

"So it's a deal?", Patrick asks excitedly.

Slowly nodding their heads, Cindy and Janice extend their hands before them.

Shaking their hands with enthusiasm, Patrick says, "Oh! I think you'll be needing this as well."

Snapping his fingers, a small business card appears in his hand. Offering it to the models, he replies, "Here be the address of the hotel I'll be checking into, as well as the address and time of the design audition tomorrow. 3pm sharp. Don't be late! Now if you don't mind, I've had a really long travel and would like to get a good night's sleep fer tomorrow. Ta-ta ladies!"

Then with a snap of his fingers, Patrick disappears in mid-air. Looking at each other again, Janice says, "Did that really just happen?"

Shaking the bag of coins in her hand, Cindy says, "Uh-huh. You know what this means?"

Smiling devilishly, Janice and Cindy pound on the trailer door and yell in unison "WE QUIT!"

* * *

Re-materializing at his hotel lobby, Patrick walks up to the guest services counter and says, "Checking in please."

Not noticing anyone there, the hotel guest clerk looks around in confusion.

"Down here!", Patrick says.

"I'm so sorry sir. I didn't see you down there.", the hotel clerk says apologetically.

"Not to worry", Patrick says back. "It happens all the time. I'll be needin' a room for the next couple days. Is the penthouse available?"

"I'm sorry sir, but it's already taken. There's a charity organization staying with us and they've already booked that room for a meeting tomorrow morning."

Still happy over his previous meeting with Cindy Crawford and Janice Dickinson, Patrick beams, "Well, that's fine. I'll take the best room ye got available. I'll be payin' in advance if you don't mind."

"Why sure mister…"

"Patrick Derby O'Gillian. You remember that name now. I'm gonna be famous!"

Smiling at his charm, the clerk says, "Of course Mr. O'Gillian. And how will you be paying?"

"In gold of course!"

Patrick then takes out the gold from his pocket and places it on the counter.

Shocked, the clerk says, "Um, I'm going to have to speak with my manager for a moment. We don't usually get paid in gold for rooms."

"Sure, sure.", Patrick replied. "Just don't be too long about it. I have a full day tomorrow!"

Smiling, the clerk takes the gold and walks into the back room.

Looking around the lobby, Patrick is impressed with his hotel decision. He had seen photos of the hotel in various fashion spreads of countless fashion magazines. It didn't carry the charm of a grand oak tree, but the place was immaculate and plush. The description extended to the persons in attendance as well. Several clusters of well dressed people were scattered here and there in deep conversation.

Patrick is about turn back to the desk counter when out of the corner of his eye he sees two female figures standing off to the side. Their silhouettes are no stranger to someone with his passion for design. Could it be? Yes! It is!

Standing as if their goddess-like personas were ordinary people chatting it up, Patrick sees supermodels Linda Evangelista and Vendela. Patrick is a leprechaun after all, but even HE couldn't believe so much luck was coming his way.

Using his shillelagh for balance, Patrick takes a deep breath and quickly takes advantage of the golden opportunity.

Removing his bowler hat again, Patrick bowed low to the women and said, "Forgive the intrusion but I am a student of fashion and it would be a travesty of fate to not tell both of you ladies just what a significant honor it is to be in your presence."

Blushing and surprised, the two supermodels giggle like school girls.

"My name be Patrick Derby O'Gillian and you are looking at the next future winner of Project Runway. I'm honored to make your acquaintance."

Taking both of their hands, Patrick kisses each one. He then steps aside, bows, and is ready to walk away when Linda Evangelista stops him.

"Wait! Are you here for the Feed the Hungry charity? We've never seen you at any of the meetings."

Turning back to the unearthly beautiful women, Patrick replies, "No, I'm just checking in for an audition I have scheduled in the city for tomorrow. At 3pm I'll be showing my designs to some judges for a chance to be on the next season of Project Runway."

Smiling, Vendela says, "Well good luck Patrick. We're here to help support a charity that helps feed the homeless in the city. So many families go without food every day. We're trying to get people to donate canned and non-perishable food for several different food pantries throughout the city."

Linda adds, "Every little bit helps."

"You don't say?", Patrick replies. "That sounds like a very worthwhile cause. How much food have you raised so far?"

Linda answers, "Not as much as we'd like. We collected enough food to feed half of the shelters for the next few months, but we need quite a bit more to make sure every city pantry is stocked for the rest of the year."

Scratching his head, Patrick says, "I think I have something that might help."

Taking his shillelagh, Patrick whispers a Gallic incantation and it instantly transforms into a large cornucopia horn filled with several fruits and vegetables jutting out of it. The two women's eyes widen in amazement.

"This is a magical cornucopia. Just wish for any type of food and it'll magically appear for ye. You give this to your charity leaders and those food pantries shouldn't be wantin' for anything for a long time."

He then hands a cluster of ripe grapes to the both of them. They uneasily take bites and excitedly say, "It's real! It's real!"

Smiling, Patrick hands them the cornucopia. "With my compliments."

He then bows, and turns back toward the hotel counter.

"Wait!" the two models reply. "This is SO generous! Is there anything we can do for you?"

"Well," Patrick says, "I won't hold you to it, but if you could, I would LOVE it if the both of you would consider modeling some of my sample dresses for the Project Runway audition tomorrow. I couldn't think of anyone more qualified."

"It's a deal!" Linda and Vendela immediately say in unison.

Clicking his heels in excitement, Patrick snaps his fingers and another small white business card appears. "Here's the address and time of when my audition will be held", he says. "If you could be there, I'd consider our exchange fairly met."

Patrick then hears a familiar voice say, "Mr. O'Gillian? Sir?"

Turning around, he sees the desk clerk has returned. Tipping his hat to Linda and Vendela, Patrick says, "I must be going, but I look forward to seeing both of you ladies again tomorrow. Sleep tight!"

Walking back to the counter, the clerk replies, "My manager agreed to the payment and here is the change back for the cost of the room."

Handing back several thousand dollars and a room key to Patrick, the clerk waves him off as he heads to the elevators, ready for a good night's rest.

* * *

The next morning Patrick calls the building his audition will be held at to confirm that his garments arrived safely. Satisfied with the response, Patrick has a light brunch at the hotel restaurant. The tip he gives the waitress is a bit generous, but he's in way too good a mood to not do otherwise.

Wanting to stretch his legs a bit, Patrick decides not to use magic but instead to walk to the audition location. He's never been is such a huge city after all, and wanted to get in as many sights as he could before being sequestered into the show's strict work schedule.

Along the way Patrick runs into a huge parade. Instantly recognizing the green clovers, fake pots of gold, and badly dressed versions of his fellow leprechaun kinsmen, Patrick remembers that today is St. Patrick's Day. Instead of feeling his usual sense of annoyance at having to participate in what he thought of as an out dated holiday, he instead now felt sadness and regret at how he left things with his father back home.

Among the cheers from the crowd, Patrick distinctly hears several boos and hisses directed at the colorful Irish floats moving along the central street. Intrigued at who would be so rude, he followed the negative shouts to the source.

Standing in the middle of the flocks of people gathered along the street were a group of protesters carrying signs that said things like: "Bigotry No More", "Stop the Hate", and "Acceptance Now".

Incredibly, in the middle of the protest group were none other than former supermodels Iman and Carol Alt. They are both wearing shirts that say 'Love is Love, Your Bigotry is Hate'.

Walking up to them, Patrick asks, "What are you protesting against?"

In between shouts Iman replies, "Year after year the people who organize this parade have purposefully excluded any and all LGBT people from taking part in it."

Carol chimes in with, "Yeah, even LGBT businesses who've promised to support the parade monetarily have gotten the ax. We're here to let these people know that their hated is outdated and needs to change now."

Confused, Patrick asks, "So even Irish gay people are excluded from celebrating a part of their heritage simply because of what they do in the privacy of their own homes?"

In unison, Iman and Carol say, "Exactly."

Still perplexed, Patrick says, "Where are these people living? Under a rock? Why, even in my home country of Ireland gay people have been an open part of the St. Patty's Day celebration for years now. I thought America was supposed to be a progressive nation."

"You'd think so." Carol says dejectedly.

Now angered, Patrick says, "Even me own Pa who's 312 years old knows gay people are an important part of society. This isn't right!"

Thinking they heard Patrick wrong regarding his father's age, they pass him a banner that says, "Kiss Me, I'm Gay Irish". He holds it over his head and repeats the same phrases Iman and Carol Alt blandish.

10 minutes into it an overweight man wearing a green suit walks over and says, "Why don't you bleeding heart liberals go home already? This is OUR parade and there ain't nothin' you can do to change it. The day one of them drag queens or dykes show their ugly faces on one of our floats is the day I'll eat my hat!"

Furious, Patrick says, "Oh yeah?!"

With a snap of his fingers, the suit the man is wearing in front of him instantly transforms into a large green hoop dress, his nails grow three times in length, and are coated in bright neon green nail polish. Similarly, his green penny loafer shoes become stiletto high heels, heavy make-up appears on his face, and his hair becomes a large bouffant hairdo.

Seeing the new outfit he is magically wearing, the man screams in fright.

Patrick snaps his fingers again and people on the float behind the man similarly transform. Every man on it begins to change into a green clad drag queen. Every woman on the float suddenly develops a mullet style hairdo, construction boots appear on their feet, blue jeans replace dresses and skirts, and they all are now wearing green t-shirts that say 'Huge Dyke and Proud'.

Each time Patrick snaps his fingers, a new float similarly changes from straight-laced to gay and fabulous. The resulting shrieks of horror and panic from the parade floats are soon muffled by the roars of laughter from the countless swarms of parade onlookers.

When Patrick looks over at Iman and Carol Alt, he can't help but grin to see Carol doubled over in belly laughs and Iman literally on the floor, too filled with laughter to utter a sound for several seconds. When she finally is able to create sound again, she lets out a long stream of consistent laughter that would put any comedian's audience member to shame.

When the two of them are finally able to gain their composure again, they turn to Patrick and ask him if he's responsible for this. With a proud grin, Patrick nods his head.

"How did you do this?", Iman asks.

"Magic, me dear. Just a little leprechaun magic."

"That's amazing!", Carol Alt chimes.

"'Twas nothin'." Patrick blushes from embarrassment. "Magic spells are required learning at me school back home. It does come in handy in a pinch."

Suddenly Patrick realizes he's been sidetracked. Pulling out his pocket watch, Patrick cries out in shock.

"What's wrong?", Carol asks.

"If I don't leave now, I may be late for me audition!"

Interested, Iman asks, "Audition for what? You auditioning for a Broadway show?"

"Not quite.", Patrick says. "I'm auditioning to be on the next season of Project Runway. I've got a few models lined up and iffen I don't get a move on I'm afraid I'll miss them!"

Looking at Iman, Carol says, "Well, we can't let that happen to our hero of the day now can we. I'd be happy to fill-in if you lose any of your models."

With her hands on her hips, Iman says, "You can count me in too."

Completely flattered and beside himself, Patrick says, "I don't know how to thank you ladies. If you're ready, we can leave now."

"Lets!", the supermodels say in unison.

Before walking off, Patrick snaps his fingers one last time. When he does, the rude man who chastised him earlier suddenly has a hat in his mouth. With a fiendish grin, Patrick tells him to enjoy his meal.

* * *

When the trio of new found friends finally arrive at the Parsons building where Patrick's audition is to be held, they walk into a whirlwind of chaos. Everywhere they look, fellow designers are rushing to and fro, adjusting hem lines and making last minute alterations to their garments. Sitting off to the side are several other designers in tears over what must be assumed to have been failed auditions. When they see Patrick walk in with Iman and Carol Alt though, everyone suddenly stops in their tracks.

What appears to be a savvy building receptionist, sensing a sudden wave of fan-boy designers are about to mob the two supermodels, instantly swoops in and guides all three professionals into a newly opening elevator. The new girl immediately hits the floor 20 button and the doors begin to close, much to the disappointment of the addled designers outside.

When the elevator car begins to rise, the receptionist turns to Patrick and speedily says, "I assume you're Patrick Derby O'Gillian?"

Patrick slowly nods his head yes.

"Good.", the receptionist says. "My name is Amanda Whipcrack. I'm the personal assistant to Heidi Klum. Your other models are waiting for you upstairs in Dressing Room 7." Turning to Iman and Carol Alt, Amanda continues, "You two of course need no introduction. I've been a fan of yours for a long time now."

Smiling brilliantly, Carol and Iman slightly bow out of respect given. This makes Amanda blush.

Snapping back to attention, Amanda returns her focus to Patrick once more and says, "When the doors open, you'll find Dressing Room 7 to the left, three doors down, on the right. You're a little late so you only have 5 minutes to put your models into their garments before a team of hair and make-up artists arrive, at which time you'll only have 15 minutes for our salon professionals to work their magic. Fortunately, the ladies you've chosen to model your garments don't require much work at all." Patrick could see Amanda slightly blushing again.

"Now," Amanda continues, "once the 15 minutes are up the hair and make-up team will leave the room to help the next set of designers who have later auditions. When this happens, you and your models are to turn left down the hall and report to Meeting Room 1. It's the large double doors at the end of the hall, so you can't miss it."

At that moment the elevator doors ding open. As the cluster of people exit the elevator car, Amanda steps off to the side. "I'll let the judges know you've arrived and will be ready shortly. Good luck with your audition."

Turning on cue, Amanda heads speedily down the hall and disappears behind a large set of doors. Patrick and the models head the opposite direction, and quickly find Dressing Room 7. Opening up the doors, Patrick sees Cindy Crawford, Janice Dickinson, Linda Evangelista and Vendela already inside. Once Iman and Carol Alt see their long-time supermodel friends, a series of squeals, giggles and hugs commence.

"Oh my god! What are you doing here?"

"I haven't seen you in ages! How are you?"

"You look fantastic! You haven't aged a day!"

"Look at that body. I hate you, you bitch!"

"How are the kids? They ready for college yet?"

Overjoyed with his sheer luck, Patrick tries his best not to gush over the amazing set of women before him. Instead, he loudly clears his throat. The supermodels stop their conversations and turn their attention to Patrick.

Now knowing what Amanda Whipcrack felt in the elevator, the deeply blushing Patrick says, "First of all, I just wanted to say thank you to each and every one of you for being here. You don't know what it means to me that such globally known women of the fashion world are all here just to help me. It really does my little Irish heart proud. Now, has anyone seen my garment box of clothes?"

Several of the models look at one another nervously. Finally Cindy Crawford says, "We found your garment box, but I think there's a bit of a problem Patrick."

With his heart racing a mile-a-minute, Patrick asks, "What problem?"

Linda Evangelista then takes one of the garments out of the box and holds it up to her chest. While the garment she is holding is gorgeous and expertly sewn, the size of the dress is unfortunately leprechaun sized and thus much too small to fit any of the models present.

Laughing, Patrick says, "Oh, is that all?"

Snapping his fingers, the various dresses and shoes neatly folded in Patrick's garment box magically appear on the individual models and are suddenly sized to fit each of their frames.

The supermodels gasp, ooing and ahhing at their beautiful new clothes. Cindy Crawford is now wearing a red sequined bustier top with an expertly cut set of straight leg pair of red silk pants. Janice Dickinson is wearing an orange custom turtleneck sweater and a black patch-work leather skirt. Linda Evangelista is wearing a yellow red carpet ready evening dress with matching clutch. Vendela is wearing a green women's business suit that is a play on the traditional leprechaun costume. Iman is wearing an iridescent blue summer cocktail dress with matching bolero jacket and brimmed hat. Carol Alt is wearing a purple 60s style mod dress with matching pair of suede go-go boots. Collectively, the color pallet of the models make up a colorful rainbow that fits not only Patrick's bright flair for the dramatic, but also provides a symbolic homage to one of the most sacred images to his people.

The second the magical transformation is complete, a team of hair and make-up people burst into the room. Each model is seated at their own mirrored dress station and the new team of assistants gets straight to work. As Patrick is telling each stylist exactly how he wants his model's make-up and hair to look, he spots a familiar looking pair of shoes sticking out of a nearby rack of clothing. After all the stylists have their orders, Patrick walks directly to the hanging rack and dramatically pushes the dresses aside to see if his suspicions were correct. Sure enough, standing on the other side of the clothes rack is the owner of the pair of shoes Patrick has seen since his childhood: Patrick's father.

"Pa! What are you doin' here? Out to sabotage me only chance for success?"

With a defeated look on his face, Patrick's father says, "No son. Nothin' like that."

Suspicious, Patrick asks, "What then?"

Taking off his bowler hat, Patrick's father twists it in his hands and looks to the ground.

"I'm here to make sure my son is the best damn designer he can be."

Confused, Patrick exclaims, "What? But you said…"

Stopping him, Patrick's father says, "I know what I said son. I was a fool. A stubborn old fool. I've known the life of a leprechaun wasn't for you. I've know it since you were 64 years old! I just kept hoping that you'd change your mind and keep up the family tradition like I expected ye to. The moment I slammed that door behind me I knew I was making a mistake, so I took our special wishin' gold and made a bit of luck come your way."

With his hand to his temple, Patrick says, "Wait a minute. Are you saying that all the luck that I've been having since I arrived in New York City is because of you?"

With a bashful face, Patrick's father says, "Aye. That be right."

"Why?", Patrick asks in confusion.

Steely, Patrick's father says, "Because you're an O'Gillian! Leprechaun lifestyle or no leprechaun lifestyle, I want people to hold their head up high when they see you cross the street and say, 'that there is Patrick Derby O'Gillian, the greatest leprechaun ye ever did see!' If you want to make dresses for a living then by golly, make the best damn dresses you can! And if it takes a little magic to make sure my son gets his foot in the door, then you can bet by blarney that I'll be doin' it!"

Sympathetic, but still upset, Patrick says, "Pa, if you charm those judges to think my designs are something other than they are, then I've already lost before I've even started!"

Putting his hand on his son's shoulder, Patrick's father says, "No son. That part I've not cast a lick of magic on. Once you walk through those judges doors, the rest is up to you. I believe in ye son. I know you can do it. I just want to make sure those fool headed judges know that they're not dealin' with no rank amateur."

Now teary eyed, Patrick embraces his father like he's never done before.

"I'm proud of ye son."

"I love you dad."

A few seconds into their embrace, the two leprechauns hear a loud set of sniffles. Turning around, they see that everyone in the room has a tissue in their hands and is dabbing away large crocodile tears from their eyes.

Iman says, "That's so beautiful."

One of the stylists says, "Yeah, and thank god for water-proof make-up."

The lead stylist then says, "Shit! We have to be in Dressing Room 3 like now! Everyone, gather your items and let's head out."

Once the swarm of stylists leave, Patrick is amazed to see all of his models left behind are pristinely accessorized with perfect make-up and hair. His little leprechaun heart leaps for joy within him.

"Alright ladies, this is it! I hope all of you are ready."

The gaggle of models murmur their confirmation to one another in solidarity.

"The luck of the Irish to ya!", Patrick's father shouts.

Smiling, Patrick turns to him and says, "Thanks Pa."

The models line-up at the door and march out single file towards the large double doors at the end of the hall. Inside of him Patrick thinks to himself, '*Eat your heart out Tom Ford!*'

APRIL

APRIL FOOL'S DAY:
"APRIL FOOL"
BY ALAN SMITHEE

"Hey Janet, can I talk to you a moment?"

Annoyed beyond belief, the blonde human resources director waves in Henry as she goes over several stacks of paperwork on her desk.

Still looking down, Janet says "I hope it's not another complaint about the crazy shenanigans you and your co-workers have been pulling today. I understand that it's April Fool's Day, but seriously, I'm not paid enough money to put in all these crazy requests today."

"Like what?"

Holding her hands to her temples, Janet replies "Barry in Accounting thought it would be funny to leave a dribble glass for Arlene in Payroll to drink from. It worked but Susan in IT slipped on the puddle it left behind so now I have to process a Worker's Comp claim. Then Larry in Research told Gordon that his dog died. Well, Gordon was in tears which made Larry feel bad so he admitted that it was an April Fool's joke. Evidently Gordon didn't think it was funny so he put in a complaint of emotional distress. THEN Barbara in Customer Service thought it would be funny to eat several person's lunches in the communal refrigerator, then leave a Post-It note on each empty tray marked 'needs salt'. And don't get me started on this morning's meeting when the CFO tried leaving a whoopee cushion on the property owner's chair. Needless to say, she was NOT amused. Seriously, I know that everyone here are adults, but my 3 year old has more maturity than most of the people here today.

Henry takes a seat.

"Sorry to hear it. Actually, I wanted to talk to you about my health benefits. I'm going through a divorce, see, and I wanted to know how long I can carry my wife's coverage before it expires."

Janet stares at Henry dead eyed. "Not funny Henry."

"I'm not kidding! We've been going through some problems for some time now. The final paperwork should go through next week."

Reaching into her drawer, Janet pulls out a bottle of aspirin and an Evian water bottle. Gulping down the pills, she chases it down with a mouth full of water and wipes her mouth dry.

"Out."

Confused, Henry asks "Excuse me?"

"You heard me. I just told you that I don't have time for any more foolishness right now, but in you come anyway and give me some awful story. One: it's not funny. Two: I can't believe you'd say such a horrible thing about Betty. And three: tell all your other little friends out there that I had better not have any more craziness come into my office for the rest of the day if they know what's good for them!"

"But I'm not making it up. I'm really going through a divorce."

"Mmm-hmm. I'll tell you what. You said that your divorce isn't going through until next week, right? Come back on Monday and if you still plan on divorcing your wife of 16 years, we'll go over your benefit options then. Capisce?"

"But..."

Janet takes Henry by the shoulders and lifts him up from his chair.

"Put, put... Monday."

Guiding Henry to her door, Janet adds "Now go back to your office and think about what a horrible thing you just said and how Betty would feel if she heard you say it."

"But..."

Holding the door in hand, Janet continues "Divorce. Honestly."

With that she closes the door on Henry, leaving him standing alone in the hallway.

Utterly dumbfounded, Henry is forced to head back to his office to continue with the forecast report due at the end of the day. Along the way Henry is hit from behind with a ball of paper. Turning around, he spots Barry leaning back in his office chair with a huge grin on his face.

"So who kicked your puppy?"

Absently, Henry asks "What?"

Laughing, Barry repeats "I asked who kicked your puppy. You look as if your about to jump out of a window or something."

Walking over to Barry's open doorway, Henry says "I just got back from Janet's office. She thinks I was pulling an April Fool's prank but I wasn't."

Still laughing, Barry says "She got me this morning too!"

"Yeah, I heard about your dribble glass incident." Henry states. "Pretty funny."

Now near tears, Barry says "You should have seen Susan fall on her back. It's probably the first time in decades that woman's legs have been up in the air!"

Weakly smiling, Henry manages to let out a few forced chuckles.

"So what were you trying to pull over on Janet?"

"I wasn't trying to pull over anything. I told her that I was heading for a divorce and that I needed to go over some benefit options with her."

Slapping his leg, Barry says "Divorce? Good one Henry! I bet that got 'ol Janet flustered."

"It did. She told me to leave and come back later, when it isn't April Fool's Day anymore."

Putting his hands behind his head, Barry asks "So what were you gonna tell Janet you were getting a divorce over?"

Henry kicks the doorframe repeatedly with the tip of his shoe. "It's personal."

"Oh come on, you can tell me."

After a few moments Henry says "I've met someone else."

Now sitting up in his chair, Barry says "You old dog you!"

"Well it's not something that I'm proud of. I've been married to Betty for a long time and I still love her. It's just one of these things that happened."

Grabbing a pen, Barry waves it around the air several times dramatically saying "Poof! You're divorced!"

Henry rolls his eyes and heads back down the hall towards his own office. After a few minutes of working on the forecast, there's a knock at the door. Looking up, Henry sees Mason from Research.

"I just talked to Barry and he told me you're getting a divorce. Is that true or are you just pulling an April Fool's joke on him?"

Sighing, Henry says "It's not a joke. The divorce will be final this time next week."

Coming in and sitting in front of Henry's desk, Mason exclaims "No way!"

"Way."

"Barry didn't tell me what the divorce is over. What happened?"

Ashamed and slightly embarrassed, Henry looks out the window for a moment before he finally gives into to Mason's curiosity.

"Do you remember that work meeting we flew to Vegas for a couple months ago?"

"Hell yeah I do! Best Vegas weekend ever! Of course, most of that trip is a booze filled haze."

"Well, do you remember how I went missing for the second day into it?"

Guffawing, Mason shares "Boy was Janet and Bill angry about that one. They didn't know whether to fire you or send out a search party."

"Yeah, well, I met someone the previous night and we just hit it off right away."

Wide eyed, Mason says "You've gotta be kidding me!"

"Nope. It's true. It's not like I went out looking to have an affair on my wife. There I was, playing some slots when one of the cocktail waitresses hands me a drink. I told her that I didn't order anything, but she told me that it was compliments of one of the high rollers across the way. I introduced myself, one thing led to another, and before I know it we're spending the next 24 hours together. It was amazing."

"Wait a second, you're telling me that the reason why you're getting a divorce is because you have some rich Vegas lady stuffing cash down your pants? You almost had me there for a second."

"It's not exactly that…"

Getting up from his chair, Mason disappointedly says "No high roller is gonna send a drink to some schmoe pulling slots on a casino floor and then shower them with their attention for the rest of the weekend. If that were the case, I'D have 10 sugar mommas of my own by now."

"But…"

Shaking his head, Mason concludes "If I were you I'd think of another April Fool's story. That one just doesn't hold water."

Mason then walks out of the room, leaving Henry to ponder if he still has his own sanity or not. Looking at the clock, Henry sees that it is just past three o'clock. Shifting his thoughts back to work, he continues working on the business forecast and loses track of time.

Once it is finished, Henry looks at the clock again. Four thirty. Suddenly the long work hours get the best of him, forcing him to submit to a long yawn. He hits 'save' on his computer monitor, then e-mails the document to the necessary co-workers. Slumped in his chair, Henry looks out the window again and sees that the sun is starting to set. Slowly he turns off his computer, collects his wallet and cell phone from his computer drawer, then grabs his coat to leave for the day.

He's about to enter his car in the stacked parking structure when he hears a familiar voice.

"Henry!"

Looking behind him, Henry spots Joan, the office busy body, walking toward him carrying her trademark briefcase.

"Hey Joan. You heading out too?"

"Yeah, but what's this I hear about you and Betty getting a divorce? Barry and Mason swear it's an April Fool's joke, but if it is one, I'm here to tell you it's not very funny."

With eyes now to the ceiling, Henry sighs again, allowing his shoulders to slump. Slowly turning to face Joan again, Henry says "It's not an April Fool's joke and believe me, I KNOW it's not funny at all. It's just what is."

"So it's true?"

"Yeah, it's true."

Confused, Joan interjects "Mason said that you're leaving Betty for some rich lady from Vegas."

"Mason read more into the story than what was actually said."

Setting her briefcase against her leg, Joan crosses her arms and asks "So what's the truth?"

Eyeing Joan, Henry realizes that he knew this moment would come eventually. Almost relieved that part of his burden can now be shared, Henry tells Joan "I'm not leaving Betty for some rich lady from Vegas. I'm leaving Betty for a man I met in Vegas who actually lives here in L.A. That's why we're getting a divorce. Betty left me because I finally admitted to her that I'm gay."

Joan's mouth slowly opens in shock.

"You're gay?"

Throwing his coat on top of his car, Henry answers with a simple "Yeah, I'm gay."

Stopping to think about it a moment, Joan finally says "Wow. This is so sudden. I'm sorry that it took you this long to finally admit it. To be honest, I've had my suspicions but you and Betty seemed so happy together. This must be hard on the both of you."

"You have no idea. I'm leaving the house to Betty in the divorce. I was gonna rent an apartment near work, but Bradley, that's his name, insisted that I move in with him. I'm really falling for this guy but in all honesty it's all happening a little too fast for my taste. He's beautiful, wonderful to be around, and is so far everything I could ever want in a guy. The thing is, I don't know if I'm rushing in too quickly or if I should just let things happen. I'm kind of lost emotionally at the moment."

"Do you think Bradley loves you?"

A warm soft smile goes across Henry's face. "I think so. He's said so on a couple occasions and I think I do too. I mean, I'm leaving my wife to be with him so that's gotta account for something, right?"

Now smiling back, Joan says "That's something only you'll be able to answer for yourself Henry. You know, I'd like to think we're more than just co-workers. If you ever need an ear or shoulder to lean on, I'm always here."

Joan walks over to Henry and gives him a strong hug. Sincerely, Henry says back "Thanks Joan. I really appreciate that."

Letting go, Joan takes a step back and looks into Henry's face. "So, what does your new beau do? Are you gonna show him off to us or are you going to keep him all to yourself?"

Suddenly Henry gets an uncomfortable look on his face. "I don't think I'm ready to cross that bridge yet. I think I want my divorce to finally cool down before I even think about putting on the dog and pony show."

"Of course! Of course!" Joan exclaims. "I was just wondering. Well, congratulations. I gotta get going. Drive safe and I'll see you tomorrow morning!"

As Henry watches Joan rush over to her car, he can almost see the thought bubbles forming over her head of which co-worker she's planning to call first with the juicy gossip.

Finally reaching Bradley's elaborate Hollywood Hills home, Henry hits the open button on his car visor. The large security gate slowly moves inward in response, allowing Henry to cross it's threshold. Driving up the long driveway, Henry notices the evening sprinklers have turned on automatically, giving the lush landscape surrounding him a wondrous shine.

Hitting another button, the rich redwood garage doors open. Henry parks, grabs his things, hits the garage door button again, and heads for the door leading into the stately manor.

Punching the series of necessary numbers on the security panel, Henry lets himself in, throwing his coat on a nearby chair. Once upstairs, he draws a hot bath, adding the contents of a nearby container into the rushing water. Soon the bath is filled with both hot water and foaming bubbles. He lights some candles for an added spa effect.

Pealing out of his work clothes, the long day behind him is slowly dropped from his person one article of clothing at a time. When fully nude, he slips in to the water. Suddenly his burdens dissolve into the hot water jets around him. He smiles in ecstasy. Opening his eyes, Henry spots Bradley's *International Man of the Year* award displayed on a nearby shelf. He then looks over at the assorted array of expensive colognes and various hair and skin products neatly lined up along either side of the main vanity. A clothes dresser form holds a tuxedo, no doubt for Bradley to wear at an upcoming event.

Completely at peace, Henry starts to nod off, leaning his head back onto the built-in head rest. After a few minutes, Henry is awakened by a set of strong hands gently massaging his shoulders and neck. He looks upward into the face of the man he's been waiting all day to see. Bradley's blue eyes sparkle radiantly as he looks upon the man who's been on his mind all day as well. The two of them gently kiss.

"You just get in?"

"Mmm-hmm. I was afraid to wake you. You looked so relaxed. Long day at work?"

Smiling, Henry says "Yeah. April Fool's Day is a pretty big deal at the office. But I did manage to get some work done. How about you? How was your day?"

Bradley wraps his arms around Henry's neck and chest, completely uncaring that he's getting wet in the process. He rests his cheek against the side of Henry's head.

"Well, the shoot ran longer than I expected but at least I got along with the new cast and director. Have you had dinner yet?"

Completely forgetting about his appetite, Henry is suddenly aware of just how hungry he is.

"No. You?"

"They had some pizza and lasagna in the commissary but it didn't look all that appetizing. What do you say we order in some Chinese food and watch a really bad horror movie?"

Completely content, Henry smiles and says sarcastically "That'll be perfect. So, what'll it be? The Hangover? Limitless? No, wait…you said horror. The A-Team it is."

Knowing he's being royally ribbed, Bradley jumps on top of Henry, fully clothed and all. Not caring that his clothes are now officially soaked, Bradley smiles directly into Henry's face and says, "You're seriously asking for it, aren't you?"

Once Henry stops laughing, he begins gently finger twisting Bradley's bangs.

"For as long as you'll have me."

"Good, because I wouldn't want it any other way."

With a raised eye brow, Henry asks, "April Fools?"

Still looking directly into Henry's face, Bradley sweetly says, "No, just the honest truth.

EASTER:
"BUNNY TRAIL"
BY JON MACY

MAY

MOTHER'S DAY:
"CHARLIE'S SONG"
BY MITCHUM SINCLAIR
AND SALVADOR HERNANDEZ

S till there was the music. No matter what was happening with Charlie, he had his music. It was there to encourage him, comfort him, love him, and yes, even scold him on occasion. For years, music understood him the way no person could...

Charlie rolls out of the hotel bed, wishing there was an iPod dock so he could begin his morning routine with some Gnarls Barkley. Instead he showers in silence, the music only in his head. Stepping out, he looks at the naked form lying on the bed. Last night's conquest: Steve? Gary? It really didn't matter. He'd stopped caring about names a long time ago. They were just playthings, and extension of the music that made him feel good. Like a .99 cent download from iTunes, catchy, pleasurable, and deletable.

Finishing up his morning ablutions, Charlie nudges The Single awake, 'Hey Handsome, wake up. I gotta leave, and so do you.' The Single rolls over, revealing a perfectly chiseled face, a physique that would rival Apollo, and hair that looked good even when mussed by nocturnal activities.

'Dude, what time is it? I got classes at 10.' College boys, why did every sentence start with 'Dude?'

'It's almost 9, you need to leave.' Charlie had a tendency to become brusque and detached the morning after. It helped him keep his distance. He tied his tie around his neck, and slipped his arms into his vest. His transformation from nighttime hedonist to respected writer was almost complete.

'Dude' (again) 'You're not gonna tell my girlfriend are you?' The Single's voice became a little high pitched.

'You really think this is all about you, don't you? I have more to lose by disclosure than you do. Rest assured your secret is safe with me. Now, please. Get up, get dressed, and get out.' Charlie's patience was at an end. He needed Bradley, (yes, that was it, BRADLEY) to leave. He was due in his publisher's office in half an hour and he still had something to do. Something no one should witness.

With Bradley gone, Charlie turns on his iPod, setting the buds in his ears, and cranks The Music up as loud as he can. It's his way of purging the night's activities out of his head. Not the sex, the sex, of course was amazing. It's all the other ephemera that go with the conquest: The Hunt, The Talking, The Negotiations, The After. But most annoying, is the part where you have to act like you care, that you have to get to know the guy. It really doesn't fit well with Charlie. If he wasn't so cheap, he'd probably forgo all the messy human interaction and just buy the sex. But he'd had some bad experiences that way.

The Single (Bradley? Yes.) had been an excellent lay. No matter how many times he said it, you could tell this wasn't his first time with a guy. But having no music to play in the background had forced Charlie to be more aware of The Single as a person. Music helped him compartmentalize and feel only the body over him. The sweat, the groaning, the pleasure.

His morning ritual now complete, Charlie begins the walk downtown to Random House. He's got a manuscript to deliver today. He could just email it, but like the music, hand delivering a manuscript to his editor had become a ritual. Every time he finished a book, he placed the typewritten manuscript in the same messenger bag, flew to New York, and walked it into the offices. Since every book he'd published had become a success, he saw no need to alter his routine.

It was short, this story, didn't even reach three hundred pages, he'd wanted it done already though. No way to elongate it. IMPOSSIBLE. Jimmy was dead, nothing after, clean goodbye. How Charlie hated him, the first character that didn't reflect his charm or some personal adventure of his, in fact Jimmy's penis will forever remain a mystery unlike The Single's.

"You sure it's done?" he said with a whimsical piece of chocolate forcefully following it splattering an inch away from the manuscript along with sprinkle of saliva.

Charlie didn't answer.

"If you have to be somewhere…" a tiny flame of hope came alive when he shut the manuscript and looked up, "…it's no big deal, and you can email me if you have any questions." Charlie's patience was up; he was like a claustrophobic man trying to find a way out.

"Nah, just checking how much time left until lunch" Chad said, as he took one more repulsive bite of that X-Large Snickers bar, gliding almost half of it in his mouth, leaving his lips drenched brown, then swallowing it clean with his tongue. He re-opened the manuscript and began reading.

How could some humans be ignorant to an impatient person in front of them?

As Chad kept on, Charlie pulled out an earphone, sliding one in, and suddenly his appearance wasn't so horrid.

Chad was just another in a long line of junior editors who would cut their teeth on a Charlie Stewart manuscript. Charlie was sure Chad would come back with the usual suggestions:

'Can we look at making Jimmy a little happier?'

'Is it really necessary to end on such a down beat?'

'I think this whole chapter on his childhood could be re-written.'

The fact of the matter was that in 15 books, 85 short stories, and countless ghost writing assignments, Charlie had never taken an editor's suggestions to heart, and yet he was revered in literary circles. So Charlie just waited in the outer office, the music soothing him, while Chad read "The Sad (and Almost True) Story Of Jimmy the Hustler".

An hour later, as the strains of #40 on the playlist were blaring into the earbuds, Chad emerged.

'It's so simple and elegant. I love it, but it's too short. We need to expand it. I have this great idea about Jimmy's brother moving to the city and taking up hooking! We can insert it into the flashback scene. That way, Jimmy's brother can discover the killer and save him! It's perfect!' Chad was waving the chocolate smeared manuscript around like it was a flag in a parade.

Charlie stared at Chad in disbelief. No, he would not let that happen to Jimmy. As much as he despised Jimmy during the writing of this story, he was still the property of Charlie Stewart. Charlie would not allow this overweight, sweaty Neanderthal to molest Jimmy that way. Jimmy may have been a pain in the ass, but he still had his dignity. Charlie walked up to Chad without a word, grabbed the manuscript and walked out the door.

Walking down 5th Avenue, Charlie cranked up the music. He needed soothing. He began to scroll down the playlist, trying to find the one song that would calm his nerves. But all the music sounded wrong, discordant. Instead of helping him, the music had abandoned him. Frustration welled up, he walked faster and faster, not knowing where he was going, the music mocking him. He yanked the buds out of his ears and sank down to the sidewalk, tears streaming down his face. What the Hell just happened?

He had taken criticism before, some of it worse than what Chad had just suggested. Why was he so protective of Jimmy? Jimmy had been the toughest character to write. Charlie didn't even like him, he just sprung fully formed into Charlie's mind one day, and demanded that his story be told. Charlie sat there on the sidewalk for an hour and re-read the manuscript. It was good the way it was. No, it was damned near perfection! Jimmy wasn't about to get a fucking brother, and he sure as Hell was not getting a reprieve from his death sentence. FUCK CHAD. Charlie had some ideas. He got up, dusted himself off and walked back to the hotel. Time to call his agent, and find out if he could shop this around. Then a call to Ted at McSweeney's. And tonight? Tonight it was time to download a new Single.

Charlie once knew this man, twice his size, but one of those fellows that, if allowed, can read your entire personality. The only person Charlie had dared call 'somebody' after the 'just sex' talk. His story is a twisted perfect reality, one in which Charlie had the pleasure in living in for exactly 141 days.

Somewhere near night #125, he shared his secret with Charlie. He invited Charlie to dinner at his place for the first time. Charlie knocked on the door at the appointed time, and as the door opened he saw a small girl, hair as red as Aileen Quinn. She reached over to give Charlie a handshake.

'Come in, please,' she said. She was such a fragile figure, and yet Charlie couldn't afford to pay her a look in the eye. His vision stayed on the thin ripple that outlined her pompous lips, just as her father's were.

'Well, hello there, what's your name?' Charlie's voice grogged, mostly mumbled as he tried to piece together the impact of what he was seeing.

'Shae' she said, brushing her already affectionate ripples back away from her face. Charlie looked for freckles but none were spotted.

'Do you think that's a pretty name, Shae?' She nodded, maybe a couple seconds too long, and did what her only other possible option was...ask his name.

'Charlie...what do you think about that name?' She shrugged.

'So how old are you, Shae?' She chuckled, no, rather laughed, facing down, with that scrawny, white hand pinching her lip. The laugh of embarrassment. One more brush back of her extended, broken off curls.

'My dad just wanted to let you know dinner was ready,' she said and backed away telling him it was good to meet him.

He smiled as Shae plastered her face deep into his small but proud belly. Charlie continued sitting there, embarrassed, as if he were recovering from a wet slap thrown across his face.

'Shae, eh?' Charlie finally said as he rubbed his clammy hands against his faded jeans.

'How about you just come to dinner...unless you want to walk out now?' the father said, forcing each finger to stay in place and maintaining his foot steady as he leaned against the doorway.

'How old is she?'

'9. An innocent nine year old whom you just asked if she liked her name or not,' he said chuckling, changing his position, now fully supported by his full, robust thighs.

Charlie shook his head and scratched the ripples in his forehead.

'Just don't tell me the mother's here.'

Charlie tried to force the thoughts of Night #125 from his head with the distraction of a Double Download. You would think twins would take all of his attention and concentration, but still his mind would wander back to Shae's father. As Thing One and Thing Two slept peacefully, Charlie sandwiched between them, he lay there staring at the ceiling, seeing Shae and her father, laughing and talking at the dinner table. They shared a secret language, known only to the two of them. At first it had alienated Charlie, made him feel like an outsider. Gradually, he began to realize this dinner was his introduction to what a family could be, and what he could have if he chose to. Shae's father was inviting him deeper into his life; he was showing Charlie a part of him kept hidden from all the other men. It excited, and frightened Charlie.

The next morning, Charlie (sans twins) checked out of the hotel, packed his bags, and boarded a flight for San Francisco. Ted at McSweeney's had signaled an interest in Charlie's story, and wanted him to meet up with the editors there. Charlie desperately needed to leave New York. It was now the scene of humiliation. On the flight to SFO, he resisted the urge to 'fix' his story. New York be damned, he knew it was one of his best. Instead he got a little drunk on Bloody Marys and slept.

San Francisco was so much more than a gay mecca. It was an art and cultural center all its own, with a unique vibe, so different than New York. Charlie spent the day taking in the various bookstores, coffee houses, and art centers. Wandering the city alone all day made him feel alive. In the record store he discovered new music, San Francisco music. From now on, this would be his San Francisco playlist, this music forever entwined with this city. His mood lifted to new heights, his confidence restored, Charlie took in a sumptuous dinner and retired to the hotel, alone. He was comfortable with himself today and saw no need for company.

Between Night #125 and #138, Shae and Charlie became inseparable. Charlie would spend the morning writing and be done around the time Shae got home from school. They would spend the afternoon at museums, candy shops, toy stores, and most importantly, libraries. Rather than set her loose in the children's section alone, Charlie would walk with her, perusing the books.

They would discuss why she wanted to read this book instead of that book. Charlie introduced her to the worlds of Narnia and Watership Down. They read together until her father got home and cooked dinner. They would sit around the table and discuss the events of the day: from Charlie's writing to Shea's math problems, to the things that happened to Shea's father at the office. As her father sipped his scotch in the study, winding down from the day, Charlie would tuck Shae in with a bedtime story. It was always 'Miss Suzy,' the tale of a squirrel and her toy soldier friends. It wasn't long before Charlie began to realize he was falling in love, with Shea. Her father was great, but really no more exciting that an extended play record. Sooner or later, the music would run out, and it would be time for another download. Charlie had been keeping the download urges in check, but it was only a matter of time.

Meeting a prospective new publisher is nerve wracking enough, but Charlie was feeling especially vulnerable. He had, after all, just walked out on a 20+ year relationship with Random House. It was the only commitment he'd been able to make in his life, and now it was over.

All the big guns were sitting around the conference table. You could see them salivating at the chance to work with Charlie Stewart. Behind their hungry eyes, however, you could see the worry. What had just happened to make Charlie come to them? Was this a real audition, or was Charlie using them to barter with Random House?

'As you can see, Mr. Stewart, McSweeney's is a smaller, but hipper operation. We're not going to be able to give you the kind of advance you are used to, nor the print runs bookstores expect from a Charlie Stewart novel,' Ted concluded as their meeting wrapped up.'

'I'm not really concerned with print runs, Ted. I want to have an editor I can trust. I have a very special story with me, a short story. It's imperative that my vision be honored. I want people to see Jimmy the way I see him. He deserves that much. Can you do this for me?'

'Of course, Charlie. I'll do the editing myself. I want to make sure you are happy here at McSweeney's.'

Rather than look pleased, Charlie's face drained of color. Ted was going to do the editing himself.

Charlie was lying in bed with Shae's father, listening to the steady rhythm of his breathing.

'What happened to Shea's mother?'

Shea's father involuntarily spasmed, for just a brief second.

'She died. Cancer. Shea doesn't even remember her. I don't know if that is a curse or a blessing.'

'She's a remarkable young girl. You've done a great job by yourself.'

'How's your next book coming?'

Now it was Charlie's turn to stiffen.

'Rough. I've hit a block and I don't know what to do next. I've thrown out everything I've written for the last week. Every time I get an idea, it crumbles around the weight of the story, and I can't stop thinking about it.'

'Let's see if we can distract you...'

Not knowing what else to do, Charlie stayed in San Francisco as Ted and the gang worked on Jimmy. Instead of trying to get Charlie to expand Jimmy into a full length novel, it was decided to include him in the next Quarterly Concern, due to be released in 3 months. That didn't give them a lot of time to edit the piece. Rather than trying to change the story, or add things that didn't belong, Ted focused on enhancing the story by improving the structure of the story itself. Ted and Charlie began to have business dinners.

On the plus side, Charlie got to sample some of the finest restaurants in the Bay Area. On the downside, Ted was always there, keeping the conversations strictly business.

'I don't think we need this bit of backstory. Jimmy's dialogue thoughts in the story already give the reader a very good idea of who he is and where he comes from. It also keeps Jimmy a little more mysterious.' Charlie didn't know which was worse: Ted editing his story or Ted being right. What did bother Charlie was Ted's inability to be social at all. Everything was McSweeney's and Jimmy. Ted wouldn't talk about home, office gossip, nothing. It was maddening to Charlie.

Charlie was still struggling with his novel. He spent days writing and re-writing, throwing out, and starting again. The more frustrated he became, the more he felt the walls of their home closing in. He spent less and less time with Shae, and more and more time locked in his office trying to unlock his story.

He needed a break. He looked at the clock. An hour before he needed to pick Shae up from school. Just enough time for a walk around the park to clear his head.

He walked up and down the streets, taking in the sights, but really thinking out his novel. He was so absorbed he nearly ran into the young man trying to get his attention.

'Hey!'

'Oh sorry! I was just...eh...walking.'

'Nice day for it.' The young Hispanic's eyes sparkled with adventure. 'Going anyplace special?'

'No, just clearing my head.'

'My place is just around the corner, how about some head to clear your head?'

Charlie wordlessly followed him around the corner. The downloading had begun. It was Day #140.

Charlie woke up, and immediately noticed it was dark outside. 'SHIT!' He fumbled for his clothes, and ran out the door without even a thank you or goodbye. He didn't even bother going by the school, he knew he was too late. Walking through the door, he saw Shae's father, sitting in the blacked out living room, a scotch in his hand. He looked up.

'She cried herself to sleep. She wants to know what she did to make you forget about her. She thinks this is her fault.' He appeared so calm, but the cracks in his voice betrayed the rage, bubbling just under the surface. Charlie just stood there, not knowing what to say.

'You know, its one thing to fuck around behind my back, but I can deal with it on my own. But to ignore Shae for days and then fucking LEAVE HER AT SCHOOL???!! She loves you, Charlie. She asked me if you were her other daddy!'

Charlie didn't move.

Shae's father threw his scotch at Charlie, 'SAY SOMETHING GOD DAMMIT!' The tumbler wildly missed Charlie and crashed into the television. 'Get out.'

Charlie packed his bags quickly and quietly. He left without waking Shae, or looking at her father. It was better this way.

Ted and Charlie were dining one last time to go over the latest revisions to Jimmy before putting him to bed. Although the working relationship had been icily professional, Charlie had to admit that Ted made Jimmy's story more compelling. It was one of the more rewarding editing jobs that had been done on his work. He was so happy, he was into his third cocktail by the time the entrees arrived. Ted just nursed his scotch.

'I think this is it, Charlie. You should be very proud of this story. McSweeney's is very proud to be publishing it.'

Charlie was all smiles. 'Ted, you did a great job and I am so happy to be here with you.' He reached out to grab Ted's hand. Ted drew away.

'Shae still asks about you, Charlie. It's been over a year, and still, she wonders about you.'

Charlie sobered up immediately. 'I don't even know how to respond to that.'

'Of course you don't, Charlie. You never did. It's all about you, and everyone around you suffers. You never deny, but you never apologize, never accept responsibility. She worshipped you. Fuck it, I worshipped you...I still do.'

Charlie looked, really looked into Ted's eyes. Everything Ted was saying was true. 'Ted, I truly am sorry. I never meant to hurt you and I cannot bear to think about what I did to Shae. I can't even think about her it hurts so much. I don't even know how to fix this, I've never tried to fix anything before. It's better just to leave this alone, and walk away. This album is finished, the songs are gone.'

'Fuck off with your music analogies, Charlie. Did it ever occur to you that there are other constants in life besides music? Our first album may be over, but that doesn't mean we can't record a follow up album, together. I just need you to pick up your instrument!'

Charlie and Ted caught the unintended joke at the same time. Charlie was smiling, and for the first time since Charlie walked into the McSweeney's office, Ted was too.

'Ted, I love you, I love Shae. I thought we could be a family, but I don't even fucking know how to be a family. I screwed up, and I don't know how to fix it, but I want to.'

Ted looked at Charlie, a mischievous grin on his face. 'Don't you have a room upstairs?'

They took things slow. Charlie stayed in his hotel room. Ted didn't tell Shae anything and would not let Charlie see her for months. There were fights, there were screw ups. Tempers flared, but they persevered. Ted had the patience of Job as Charlie navigated the waters of boyfriend, fiancée, and eventually husband. He adopted Shae, and began to settle in, knowing that every day was a new track on that follow up album Ted offered him.

'Wake up, Daddy Charlie!' Shae was right in his face with a plateful of pancakes.

'What's all this?' Charlie asked.

'Well, Dad and I have always celebrated Father's Day with French Toast in bed. I know you're not a girl, but you need a special day too. Do you mind if I make you pancakes on Mother's Day, just for the two of us?'

Charlie picked Shae up and held her tight. 'No, darling not at all. Happy Mother's Day to me.'

JUNE

TONY AWARDS®:
"ANTOINETTE PERRY IS A FRIEND OF MINE"
BY ROBBIE TURSI-MASICK

Four ago months, if you told me that I was not only going to have an amazing boyfriend but that I would have been seat-filling for the Tony Awards, I would've laugh at your face and then cried because those two things seemed nearly impossible.

But here I am, on the Long Island Rail Road on my way into Penn Station on the phone with my movie nerd boyfriend, Josh, as he tries to calm me down and not let me jump off the next bridge the train crossed.

"What if I trip and fall on my face in front of Bernadette Peters?!" I whispered/screamed into the receiver, making the woman across from me look up from reading '50 Shades of Grey' and scowl at me. I mouthed the words "Sorry" and "good book" with a thumbs up and eye roll.

"You're going to be fine," Josh said calmly. "They're normal people like you. Actually, you're not normal but that's beside the point."

"Joooosh," I whined.

"I'm kidding," he said with a smile. "Just don't lose your shit."

"Oh, come on," I said. "You're telling me if you sat next to Martin Scorcese at the Oscars, you wouldn't lose *your* shit? Please. They'd be mopping up your liquid form into a bucket."

He didn't say anything for a few seconds meaning that he knew I was right. "Shuddup," he finally said.

"Thank you," I responded. "Ok, I will call you when I get out of there."

"Yes," Josh said back. "And do me a favor and stay out of Patti Labelle's path in case you two get into it." He laughed.

"Lupone, Josh. Patti Lupone." I sighed. "How many times do we have to go through this? Patti LaBelle, who I love, sang Lady Marmalade and Patti Lupone was the original Evita on Broadway and is also Satan, herself."

Another pregnant pause from my nerdle. "I have no idea what you just said but have a good time."

I took a deep breath and said, "I'll try. I love you."

"Love you too, babe," he said in his husky voice and hung up.

We pulled into the train station about 6:15 which meant that I had 15 minutes to catch a taxi uptown to Radio City Music Hall and meet up with my friend Dave. He knows somebody that knows somebody that slept with some Broadway producer and was able to get us in last minute as seat fillers. Dave had explained that we basically were stationed on the sidelines and whenever someone got up to get an award or pee, we ran and sat in their seat to make the audience still look full when the TV cameras panned over the crowd. We don't get paid, which was fine by me, as long as I breathed the same air as the musical god, Stephen Sondheim.

I got out of the cab and saw Dave standing in front of the building along with some other people that I assumed were other seat-fillers. He saw me and waved me over excitedly.

I jogged over to him and gave him a hug without wrinkling either one of our suits. "So, what did I miss?" I said.

"Holy shit, Nick," he said. "You missed Neil Patrick Harris by like thirty seconds and he looked quite delish. I wish I brought my *Assassins* playbill for him to sign."

I laughed. "Don't you already have one signed already?"

"No, no. That's the *original* Broadway cast," he corrected me. "He was in the revival."

"Oh, right," I agreed with him because I didn't want to get into the details. I am a proud Broadway fan but Dave takes it to a whole other level. He has playbills and window cards covering the walls of his apartment so it pretty much looks like Sondheim, Webber and the Gerswins threw up collectively all over the place. He even has a collection of playbills that only ran fifty performances or less, just because. Yes, seriously. I won't even go into the spreadsheet he has on him at all times just in case he finds one in the middle of 7th Avenue.

A woman about the same height and color as an Oompa Loompa came out of the side door and started to speak loudly at the crowd of us. "Ladies and gentlemen, in just a few minutes, we will be escorting you into the theatre where you will be given further instructions as to where to go and what to do. At this time, please turn off any cell phones you may have and do not, I repeat, do NOT turn them on until the show is over."

Dave and I quickly took out our phones and powered them off and slipped them back into our pockets.

"After you are done, please make two lines and we will proceed into the lobby," the small lady announced. We did as we were told and walked into the building.

I remember my parents taking me to Radio City to see the Christmas Spectacular when I was younger. I thought the place was the North Pole back then, but I now realize it's even more magical then I ever thought before. People from Judy Garland to Whitney Houston walked these halls at one time or another. Music history was made here, and now I was going to be a part of just one more notch in that timeless belt.

Dave and I continued to geek out as we passed the camera crews getting ready to shoot and interview the gaggle of stars that would soon be walking the red carpet. Haven't we all wished at one time or another to hear people yell "Look here!" *click click click* "Turn around and smile!" *flash flash flash*

No, you haven't? Liar.

We stopped suddenly and the woman spoke a little softer now that we were out of the noisy New York City air. "Now, there are some rules. First off, no texting or cell phone use is allowed but you should have figured that out by now since everyone has turned them off." She looked around suspiciously at some people in the back and they went into their pockets to make sure their phones were off. She may have been small but she meant business. "With that, I hope no one brought a camera because if you are caught taking photos or videos, you will be asked to leave immediately."

Thank God, I left mine at home. Not like I could really fit it in any of my pockets because these pants were tight enough as it is and could barely fit my wallet in them. I hate getting dressed up sometimes.

"You are going to be separated in two different sections," she continued. "Half of you will be on the right and the other half on the left. When needed, one of our team members will direct you to where to sit when someone leaves their seat. If you happen to sit next to someone famous, please do not speak to them unless spoken to first. Yes, I know they're just people but we have to respect them and their personal space even if it's Hugh Jackman." Her face turned a bit red and she giggled along with a couple of other people. Maybe she wasn't such a tyrant after all. "What we do encourage is to keep a smile on your face because you never know when you might be on camera. That also means no gum chewing. You wouldn't want the world to look at you like you were a feeding cow."

Dave and I looked at each other and silently swallowed our gum.

"We are just about to start so please stay in the lines you're in now and proceed to the left or right. And most importantly, have fun." She smiled and went to talk to her co-workers.

"I'm going to shit my pants if I sit next to Cheyenne Jackson," I said to Dave as we started to move forward.

"Oh, please," he said. "You'll cream your pants way before you shit them if you sat next to him."

I slapped his shoulder jokingly as we made it to the front of the line. "Ok, I will see you out there," I said moving to the right.

"Break a leg!" he said as he went to the left.

We lined up on the side wall as the fancies started to make their way to the red seats. The girl behind me seemed to be losing her mind already and was shaking like an idiot.

"You ok?" I asked her.

She shook her head violently.

"What's the matter?"

"I'm just really excited to be here," she said, trembling. "I mean, what if I sit next to Nick Jonas?! O. M. G. I would totally throw up!"

"Yeah," I said, "that would totally suck." I looked around for someone to save me from this mess next to me. I hate so-called fans of Broadway that only know of a show if the producers decide to sell out and drop some idiotic teeny bopper, or worse a reality star. I wonder if this asshole hyperventilating into her sequined purse even knows who Ethel Merman is.

The audience was really full now so that must mean that the show was about to begin.

A guy came over with a Madonna-like headset and gave us our final instructions.

"When we need you, we will direct you to another member of our team in the theatre and they will tell you which seat to fill," he said quickly. "Sometimes we will need one but other times we will need two. Don't get comfortable out there because as soon as the person comes back, you get up and come back here. Got it?"

We all nodded.

Soon, the lights went down and the orchestra started.

The joy that went through me cannot be explained through words so I'll take you out for drinks one day to express it in person.

I was in the presence of Broadway royalty and maybe, just maybe, I'll get to sit next to them (for at least 30 seconds).

Headset guy called for us one and two at a time for the first two hours but it was mostly to sit in the back. All the real stars were up front.

When ensemble cast member number fifteen came back from her pee break, I went back to the wall. I was the only one there so I was at the front of the line as the rest of the fillers came to join me.

Twenty awards and five performances later, Headset Guy finally needed me to plop my temporary ass down somewhere else. He pointed to another Headset family member that was standing in the middle row of the orchestra section. I walked over to her and she whispered in my ear, "It's your lucky day." She pointed to the first couple of rows of seats and waved me along.

As I made my way down the aisle towards the front of the theatre, I saw the seat was 4 rows back from the stage. Even though I was walking quickly, the whole world seemed to go in slow motion when I saw who was sitting next to the empty chair.

No one could ever mistake who that tight, curly brown hair and porcelain skin belonged to.

Sitting there, talking to someone next to her (man or woman I had no idea because I was in trance and going deaf) was the Broadway Goddess, Bernadette Peters.

I stood at the end of the aisle and stared at her beauty like I was missing a chromosome. The person she was talking to (who I now deduced as a woman) must have noticed me gawking because Ms. Peters turned and looked at me, jumping a bit like I was Freddy Kruger.

"Ooh!" she yelped. "You scared me." She laughed a laugh that should've won its own Tony. "Who are you?" she asked.

For a moment, I didn't know. But I did know that I was a person. A person that was about to crap his pants.

My throat made a strange noise which she cocked her head at. "Seat. Filler," I said quietly.

"Seat Filler, huh?" she said. "Shall I call you 'Mr. Filler' or just 'Seat'?" She smiled and winked.

"Let's call him 'Seaty'!" the woman next to her said with a hearty laugh. I looked at the woman and I was certain my stomach was about to explode. Yet another Broadway deity was three feet in front of me wearing round, black glasses making her eyes look a little larger than normal but not taking anything away from her divinity. Joanna Gleason.

"Honey, it was a joke," Joanna said. "You're allowed to laugh!" She and Bernadette started to giggle like high school friends.

"And please," Bernadette said, "sit down. We don't bite." She patted the seat next to her.

I nodded my head up and down like a bobblehead and sat down with a thump looking straight ahead, afraid to look at either one of them for fear of either crying or well, crying is what I would do.

"Yeah," Joanna said, "unlike some *other* people we know."

"Please. Don't remind me," Bernadette said with disgust. "I haven't seen her yet tonight and I'm perfectly fine if I don't."

"You and me both," Joanna responded. "If I have to listen to her gloat one more goddamn time, I swear I'll her tell which two holes she can shove her Tonys into."

"Jo!" Bernadette said through stifled laughter.

My heart was racing a gajillion miles a minute because not only was I sitting in the presence of the original Witch and Baker's Wife from my most favorite musical of all time, *Into the Woods*, but I was listening to them dish about someone else.

Guess everyone on Broadway doesn't love everyone on Broadway.

"Yes, well," Bernadette said, "we all have to be nicey nice for a couple of more awards. I can't believe John left me here. Remind me not call him again for a date."

"He didn't look so hot when he got up," Joanna said. "Hope he's not passed out in the bathroom."

"No, he texted me just a couple of minutes ago," Bernadette said. "He's in bed chugging a bottle of Pepto." She nudged my right shoulder lightly but I didn't move. "Guess your my date for the rest of the night, Seat." I gulped loudly

"Kid," Joanna said. "Hey Seaty!"

I broke my focus off counting the boards in the stage to look at the two of them.

"Umm..." I said, "yes, ma'am?"

"Ooh, don't call me 'ma'am,'" she said. "I still have my looks."

Fuck, I just insulted a Tony winner. Let me die now.

She reached over Bernadette and grabbed my knee. "Another joke," and she winked.

I smiled and let out a nervous laugh. "Sorry."

"It's ok," Bernadette said. "First time here?"

I nodded.

"Are you enjoying yourself so far?"

I nodded again.

"Good," she smiled. "That's all that matters."

I took a deep breath and smiled back.

"By the way, Nick," she said and I wondered how she knew my name. "Someone across the way is trying to get your attention." She pointed to my left.

I looked over and saw Dave sitting there with his hands up to his mouth saying my name over and over. I raised my hand up a bit to wave slightly and he mouthed the words "OH MY GOD" to which I mouthed "I KNOW". He then mouthed "I HATE YOU" and I stuck my tongue out.

The orchestra started up and I straightened back into my seat while the ladies settled back into theirs.

"Welcome back everyone," Neil said, "to the 98th hour of the Tony Awards." Everyone laughed at the joke even though countless people have said it before. "Only a couple more awards to give out tonight so let's get going so we can party over at Stephen Sondheim's house!"

Everyone laughed as I looked up to the big screen where a camera got a shot of his highness Stephen Sondheim smiling and shaking his finger in Neil's direction. The shot pulled back and in the top right hand corner I saw someone as white as a ghost with his knee shaking violently up and down.

Holy shit. It was me! I was three rows behind the King of the Broadway Gods! I was breathing the same air as the man who wrote the soundtrack to my life.

Bless the director for switching back to the stage because I'm sure my pale face turned green.

I sat there the rest of the night in a daze, not looking left, not looking right for fear that this was all a dream or worse it was reality and I was about to blow chunks in front of and on the majority of the Broadway community.

After Neil recapped the night's events in song, I shot up out of my seat and looked for Dave. In my Tony coma, he must have switched seats because a large man was sitting in the spot where he was a half hour ago. I pulled out my phone and turned it on. That's when I felt a tap on my shoulder. I turned to my left (and looked down) to see Bernadette Peters smiling (up) at me.

"So, Nicholas, did you enjoy the show?" She slipped on a beautiful shawl.

"Yes, Ms. Peters," I said quietly.

"Good," she said and she reached up to give my left cheek a squeeze. Normally, I hated when my grandmother did the same thing but since it was Bernadette Fucking Peters, it was totally OK.

"Bernie!" Joanna said as she quickly walked towards us, "Incoming!" and she pointed with her head to something behind us.

You know that music they play in movies when the villain is about to come on screen? It's always dark and scary just so you can be prepared for the evilness that you're about to be introduced to. Well, that's what was playing in my head when I turned to look at what was coming down the aisle towards the three of us.

My mortal enemy (even if she didn't know it or frankly cared)...Patti Lupone.

"Shit," Bernadette said under her breath but quickly plastered a smile on her face as well as Joanna.

I just stood there trying to control my sudden road rage even though I wasn't driving.

"Bernadette! Darling!" the devil said with open arms. She pulled Bernadette into a hug and they both gave each other two air kisses on both sides of their faces.

Patti finally let go of Bernadette and looked over at Joanna.

"Joanna," she simply said.

"Patti," Joanna responded. Ooh, I bet there's a story behind *that* look she just gave her.

"How are you, dear? So sorry we didn't get to see each other earlier," Patti said with her performance to date. "I was ALL the way up front with Stephen." She smiled evilly.

Bernadette simply smiled back, "That's perfectly all right. Our seats were perfectly fine back here. No distractions by loud people who can't shut up during other people's acceptance speeches." She smiled wider. Joanna cleared her throat or was that a laugh?

I swear I saw a flash of red in Patti's eyes.

OK, one for Bernie P.

"Yes, well," Patti straightened herself up taller, "They like to sit winners that have actually won something in the past *decade* closer to the stage." She smiled like Cruella De Vil at the both of them.

Ouch. That was low and Joanna looked like she was about to take her glasses off and wreck some shit. Bernadette didn't even seem fazed.

"Yes, it's very sad when people don't win awards because they were told they are too *young* to play a certain part," Bernadette retorted. "But I'm glad that didn't happen with you." She continued smiling magnificently.

She's officially my new hero of everything.

That really must've pissed Patti off because she moved closer to Bernadette's face to whisper, "Still bitter I was the better Rose and got my second Tony for it?"

"Yeah, only took you 28 YEARS to get it," Joanna said to no one in particular.

Patti turned to her. "As if you know what a second anything would look like," she said. "Well, except maybe a second husband." Joanna eyes opened wide but she said nothing in response.

"Face it," Patti the Destroyer said. "People just liked me better."

Why did my throat get itchy at that particular moment? And why did I have clear it?

Patti turned her fire eyes on me and looked startled. "Where did you come from? Who are *you*?"

She stared at me waiting for an answer to which I didn't have to because Bernadette chimed in, "This is my new friend, Nicholas. He is, well, was a seat filler tonight and also a huge fan of Broadway." She gave her a look and Patti's face changed to something slightly less crazy train and more PR.

"Oh, hello there, young man," she extended her palm down.

I took her hand and barely shook it, "Hi."

She seemed slightly insulted I didn't kiss it.

Oops.

"Have you ever seen one of my shows?" she said to me. Bernadette sighed and Joanna rolled her eyes.

"Yes," I said with less enthusiasm then I meant.

OK, I meant it.

"Oh? Which one?" Did she just bat her eyes?

"Gypsy," I answered. And unfortunately I did. Luckily it was free because it was to the invited dress rehearsal and I was forced to go with my friend Linda since her boyfriend dumped her that same day.

Damn my heart of gold.

"Ah! You see Bernadette? A fan of my TONY AWARD WINNING performance!" Patti said a little too loudly causing people to look over at us.

I stood there, quietly turning red.

"Oh, don't be embarrassed young man," Patti said. "We all get a little star struck around stars," she laughed like a crone.

"I'm not embarrassed," I said out of nowhere. That stopped the hellish cackling in its tracks but brought on the death stare.

"Excuse me?" Patti said through gritted teeth.

"I said I'm not embarrassed." I took a deep breath. "And I wasn't a fan of your performance. I preferred Ms. Peters' Rose to yours, actually and really felt that she was robbed back in 2003." I smiled like an angel.

Joanna giggled, Bernadette looked shocked and Patti look like she was about to turn into the dragon in Sleeping Beauty.

"Well," Patti huffed. "I suppose not everyone has good taste." She looked at me and the other women with venom before walking up the slope to the back of the auditorium with her handler, er, husband.

"Wow," Joanna said. "I like you, Seaty. I mean, Nick."

I stood there trying to catch my breath as Bernadette came over and hugged me.

"Thank you," she whispered in my ear and gave me a peck on the cheek.

Nope, definitely not washing that part of my body ever again.

"Good thing I didn't say I'd rather listen to Madonna singing 'Don't Cry for Me, Argentina' than her doing it," I said.

They both looked at each other and started to laugh.

"You're brave, kiddo," Joanna said. "You're lucky we're surrounded by so many people. She once punched a stagehand in the face during tech because her spotlight was off by an inch. He had to get stitches!"

I leaned back on the chair as what just transpired flooded through my very being and instantly I knew I was going to throw up.

"Excuse me," I said through my covered mouth and ran to the nearest bathroom in the lobby.

I pushed past someone (Jonathan Groff?) and slammed the stall door behind me. I dry heaved for two minutes because I barely ate anything all day. I got up off the floor and walked out to the sink. I washed my face with cold water then looked at myself in the mirror.

"You just insulted Corky's mom," I said to my reflection. "I think we should go to Disney World." I laughed and my phone started to vibrate. It was a text from Dave.

"Where the eff R U?!" it said.

"Going into the lobby now," I texted back.

The phone vibrated again, "I'm @ a bar with a cute seat filler I met when we were told 2 leave."

Leave it to Dave to hook up at the Tonys. The phone vibrated again, "Call U tmrw ;)"

I was about to respond when I heard my name being called out.

It was Bernadette and Joanna waving me over to them.

"Hello again," I said casually.

"We thought we lost you," Joanna said.

"Where's your little friend?" Bernadette asked.

"Oh, he left and," I looked at the time on my phone, "I guess I'm going to Penn Station alone."

"What? Why?" they both asked.

"I have to take the train back home,"

"Already?" Bernadette asked. "But we didn't even go to the party yet!"

I looked at her like she was speaking Chinese. "What do you mean? What party?"

"The party you are escorting us to, silly!" Bernadette said. "After all, you *are* my date for the night." She smiled lightly.

I felt the chunks again but I quickly pushed them back down. "Seriously?" I asked.

She nodded.

"You're a good kid," Joanna said. "Can't wait to see who else you'll piss off once we get some vodka in you!" She laughed then said, "Kidding!"

I was dumbfounded. "Thank you?" was all I could say.

"Don't thank me yet," Bernadette said. "Hope you don't mind getting your picture taken with us."

I shook my head, "Not at all!"

"Good," she said happily. "I think the car is here. You ready?"

"As I'll ever be," I said. "Can I just make one quick phone call? I told my boyfriend I was going to call when the show was over."

Bernadette placed her hand on her chest and gasped. "Cheating on me, already?!" She winked.

"No problem. We'll meet you outside."

"Ok!" I said a little too excitedly. I hit the speed dial and the phone rang several times before Josh picked up.

"Hewwo," he said as if he was talking into a pillow, which he probably was.

"Josh, you will NOT believe the night I had!" I said.

"OK," he said.

"And I will tell you about it all later or tomorrow but I'm going to a party right now with Bernadette Peters and Joanna Gleason. No, you don't know who they are."

"Have *yawn* fun?"

"I will. Love you!"

"Wub you too."

I hung up the phone and made my way to the exit.

I saw Bernadette and Joanna standing there, posing for the paparazzi.

"Ladies," I said.

"Ready to go?" Bernadette said.

"Yup!" I said with a cheesy grin.

"Here's the car," Joanna said.

The limo stopped in front of us and the driver came out to open the door for us. I help them both in and got in myself. I watched as the chauffeur closed the door and walked back to the front of car. When I looked in the women's direction to thank them for hundredth time tonight, I noticed they were talking to a man who I didn't see when I got in. Where he was, it was dark unlike my side of the car that picked up the street lamps' light so I couldn't make out his face but I heard a gruff voice.

"...It was actually quite hilarious," Bernadette was finishing a sentence. "Oh, and by the way. I would like to introduce you to my hero of the night."

I smiled knowing the shadow man could see me.

"This is my new friend, Nicholas," Bernadette said. The man moved forward into the light and my eyes almost fell out of their sockets as I realized whose hand I was about to shake. "Nicholas, this is Stephen Sondheim."

He grabbed my hand with his, which was soft but rough in some spots and magical all around.

"You can just call me 'Stephen.'"

I knew I should have worn Depends tonight.

FATHER'S DAY:
"FATHER'S DAY"
BY DAVID BERGER

Author's Note: Story takes place after "The Hanukkah Gift" story.

June 17, 2012

In front of the brownstone on Massachusetts Avenue guarded by vigilant oaks, Aaron Feldman sat in his car, leaning back against the headrest and staring out the windshield down the street. It was Father's Day, and he promised his mother he would stop by, but visiting home brought him back to being a teenager, back to when he had to hide being gay from his father.

When he came out, his mother thought she had failed as a parent and did what every Jewish mother does—she went into denial, thinking her son was simply overworked or under the influence of miscreants who wanted nothing more than to drag her son into darker places, like back alleys, dive bars, and bathhouses. It wasn't until Aaron finally just sat her down and said, "Mom, it's not your fault that I'm gay. I was born this way," that she started to see her boy as growing into manhood. As true as it was, he always felt that was such a cliché. And, no matter what he said, his mother would always bear the guilt of having done something while he was in the womb to have altered his DNA. Maybe she'd worn too much perfume, or played too much Mahjong, or even read too many cheesy romance novels: anything to feminize the child inside her. Years later, she finally came around, but perhaps too much around the bend, and started looking for a suitable man for her son like how one searches for the best tomato—poking, prodding, sniffing, squeezing. No gay man was safe when Sally Feldman was on the hunt, for a son-in-law, that is.

Neither the epitome of fatherhood nor the masculine ideal, Aaron's father, Jack Feldman, never addressed the issue head on. In fact, he wouldn't deal with it at all. Jack wouldn't call his son names, at least not in front of him or Sally, but he had those passive aggressive comments he'd exhale when anyone mentioned Aaron's name. As his son went through college, he would ask him if he were dating any nice girls, even though he knew the response. He felt that asking would plant the thought in Aaron's head so he'd eventually just come home one day with a new daughter-in-law, mostly to make Sally happy. Jack's concern had less to do with Aaron's happiness or Sally's peace of mind—he didn't want people judging him as a poor role model, or worse, as a weak man.

Eventually, Aaron mused, he would have to get out of the car, walk down the cement path, and cross the threshold into a tension he couldn't put into words. He didn't want to talk about anything uncomfortable, and he wasn't going to bring up Jason, the guy he'd met during Hanukkah, no matter how much his mother wanted to know. He had made the mistake of saying something to Jason while on the phone with Sally, so from that point, she just assumed they were living together. No. No talk of Jason, no matter how much he wanted to tell his parents that he was in love with a truly special man. His father would mutter under his breath, and his mother would want to invite

Jason over for dinner. Hell no. That would be a disaster of the highest degree. He stopped just before the front door, raised his hand to knock, but before he could, the door flew open and there stood his mother.

"There's my boy! Shayna punim!" Sally's Yiddish made him blush, even though he knew he would never be able to get her to stop saying things like that.

A little shorter than her son, Sally reached up to pinch his cheeks. Aaron went along with it—he didn't really have a choice.

"Hi, Mom. How are you doing?" he asked, hugging her. She always embraced him like she hadn't seen him in months.

"Oy, you know. I can't work in the garden because of my arthritis, but I get by. I have a brisket in the oven, and your sister is bringing kugel," she said, returning to the kitchen. Aaron knew better than not to follow her.

He put the bag from the bakery on the counter, and Sally peeked.

"Black and whites! Oh, you remembered!" she said, scrunching up her nose in approval. Those cookies, with half chocolate icing and half vanilla, were her favorite, and Aaron's, too.

"So, how's school? You're almost finished, right?" she said, filling a glass with iced tea and arranging some Ritz crackers on a plate around a bowl of chopped liver, both of which she placed in front of Aaron at the kitchen table.

He allowed himself a cracker and some liver, despite how bad it was for him, but he knew if he didn't eat some, he'd live to regret it later. Besides, that also gave him a few moments to think about his response. Sitting with his mother, or even his sister, he didn't mind, but the inevitable time would come when he had to say hello to his father, and that had train wreck all over it.

"Yeah, Mom. We finish June 24, and I'm ready to be done, too. This year, my students are just so incredibly lazy."

"Don't you tell me that every year?" she said, checking the oven. "Brisket's almost done. Your sister will be here around five."

A few more crackers and chopped liver. Aaron was trying to convince himself that he could make it through dinner without incident; it almost became his mantra. While his mother started regaling him with stories about her friend Hadassah's new grandson or Aunt Pesha's poodle, he wondered if he really could bring Jason here to meet his family. Surely, Jason's family had to have its own *tzouris*—drama—right? Even though Aaron thought the man was near perfect, that family had to have some issues. But, despite all the drama, he really did want Jason to be a part of his family. Six months into this relationship, and Aaron was ready for a more permanent commitment, and that also meant being a part of Jason's son, Aryeh's, life. That boy makes Jason smile so big and his eyes just light up. It had been hard for Aaron, since he's not used to being around younger children, and he didn't want to make a bad impression, especially the day they met.

• • •

Hanukkah, 2011. 11:35 p.m.

As soon as Jason and Aaron arrived at Jason's mother's house, all eyes were on Aaron. The house smelled of Hanukkah candles that had already burned out as well as oil from the potato latkes. Jason's sisters, Rebecca and Michelle, whispered to each other while looking at Aaron as their brother said hello to his parents. Aryeh had already gone to bed, exhausted from staying up to play dreidel with his grandparents. Once the introductions were over, Aaron joined Jason on the couch and asked about the man sitting with Jason's mother, Adele.

"Oh, my step-dad. Mom remarried when I was 25. He's a good man and treats my mother well. And he adores Aryeh. It's a shame he's asleep. I wanted you to meet him."

Mrs. Blumenfeld brought a plate of latkes over to the two. Rebecca quickly followed behind to hand them plates and forks.

"Sour cream or apple sauce?" Adele asked.

"Both, please," Aaron said while she put a healthy dollop of both on his plate.

Rebecca squeezed between them on the couch, nudging her brother away playfully.

"So, how'd you two meet?" she asked.

"Go easy on him, Rebecca," Jason laughed. "Aaron, I'm going to check on Aryeh. If my sister starts asking too many questions, just shove a latke in her mouth."

Not long after the inquisition started, Michelle came over and sat on the other side of Aaron. He didn't mind the questions, though, and it gave him the chance to find out more about Jason's family. Both sisters, while having similar features, had some striking differences: Michelle, the younger sister in her early 20s, had a more casual presence with a long bob of blond hair with subtle pink highlights, baby pink sweatpants and a Thor t-shirt; Rebecca, on the other hand, in her mid-30s, had French tips on her beautifully manicured nails and long, brown hair, and wore a pale blue cashmere sweater with blue slacks. Jason's step-dad, Howard, just sat in the recliner reading a novel on his Kindle, chuckling to himself about how entangled Aaron was in the third degree. He knew better than to intervene. Adele asked the girls to leave him alone and help her finish putting dishes away.

On the side table, Aaron saw a photo of Adele, her first husband, Solomon, and all three children. By the looks of it, the parents must have been in their late 20s. Jason was clinging to his father's leg, looking up at him.

Hearing Jason's shoes on the tile, Aaron turned to see him carrying a sleepy little boy, his head nestled under his father's chin.

"He heard me come in," Jason said to his mother when she gave him a look. "I had to give him his Hanukkah present."

Jason gestured with his head for Aaron to join him in the dining room, and father and son sat on a chair. Aryeh's eyes batted open a little, checking out this strange person.

"Aryeh, this is Aaron. Say hello."

The three year old buried his face in Jason's chest.

"Nice to meet you, Aryeh," Aaron said, holding out his hand.

No response. Aaron just smiled.

"It's okay, Jason. He's half-asleep." He put his hand on Jason's shoulder. "I'd be scared, too."

Aryeh never left his father's lap, although he did eventually wake up enough to eat a latke, never taking his eyes off of Aaron. Jason was right, though, about his parents: they were certainly night owls. He didn't leave until 1:30 a.m., and Jason walked him to his car. Aaron leaned back against the driver's door.

"I'm sorry about Aryeh," Jason said, leaning his forehead against Aaron's. "He was probably just tired."

"No worries. Maybe next time, we'll meet during normal daylight hours."

"I think he does like you. He's protective of me and usually throws things at people he doesn't like. You could have been wearing that latke."

Aaron gently kissed Jason's lips. "Call me," he whispered.

"Yessir," Jason said, smiling.

As Aaron drove away, he felt a little sadness, especially since he didn't remember his father being so attentive to him as a child. But, perhaps, things could change. Or not.

• • •

His mother handed him silverware and napkins to put at the table, but she kept talking about her Mahjong group or her community work at the synagogue. That woman could hold a conversation with herself quite easily. Aaron could have driven home and back, and she would still be talking, never having known he was gone. Through the front door came his sister, Rachel, kugel in hand and boyfriend in tow. Adele put the kugel on the table while Aaron said hello to his sister.

"Hey brother," she said, giving a hug and a peck. "You remember Robert." They shook hands. "Of course."

"Robert, go say hello to daddy. I need to talk to Aaron for a sec."

Rachel took her brother by the hand and led him into the living room.

"So, where's Jason?" she asked, all excited. "Robert and I were so happy when Mom said he was coming."

"Excuse me?"

"Wait. Didn't Mom ask you to bring him?"

"Uh, no. I'll bet she told Dad, he made a comment, so she said, 'Okay, okay, Jack,' threw up her hands, and relented."

Rachel pouted. "You know, you're probably right. But, she *did* mention she would ask you. That has to count for something."

Aaron shrugged.

Adele shouted, "Jack, tuck your shirt in. The kids are here, and dinner's on the table."

The last one to join the family, Jack sat at the head of the table, Adele to his left. After making the blessing over the bread, he asked Aaron what was new.

"Not much, Dad. School year's about over, so the kids just don't want to do work. But, I did find out that I'm going to that AP conference in Madrid over the summer. I think I emailed you and Mom about it."

Between mouthfuls of brisket, Jack said, "Mazal tov. They pay you to do this?"

"Yeah, I get a stipend, and all my expenses are covered. They even said I could bring a guest if I wanted."

That last part slipped out, and Aaron was afraid his father would say something. Jack just kept eating. A few mouthfuls later, he replied,

"You should take your sister with you," pointing at Michelle with his fork. "Let her see a little of the world."

"Dad! I'm sure Aaron has someone else in mind," she said, winking at her brother. Aaron glared.

Jack said, "Then don't take your sister."

Something was up. Aaron could usually count on his father to make some sort of passive aggressive remark about taking a woman with him, someone he works with perhaps. But, nothing. Robert talked about his latest client and how the blueprints he had worked so hard on for them were finally approved. Rachel chimed in that this could mean a huge bonus, maybe enough to pay for a honeymoon at some point. Aaron's sister had been talking about getting married to Robert for a few months now, but Robert felt like he wanted to wait until he had more of a steady income. He didn't want Jack and Adele to pay for it, even though that's all Adele talked about nowadays was putting together the wedding. That was sure to get Aaron's father to say something.

Jack just continued to eat, although he did nod at certain parts of the table discussion so people would know he was still there. Why wasn't he taking the bait, Aaron wondered. Surely, all this talk about a wedding would initiate one snarky remark. Maybe he *should* bring up Jason just to see what would happen? Or, maybe not tempt fate. He actually enjoyed having a comment-free conversation with his family, although he was just waiting for something happen. Rachel mentioned her start-up company was holding an auction later that month, and that just got her going on and on about it. A clothing designer, she specialized in children's wear, so she had to mention the write up about her new toddler line in the latest issue of Baby Couture.

Aaron's mind, with all the talk of toddlers, began to wander back to the first day he actually met Aryeh, awake.

• • •

A week after New Year's, Jason asked Aaron if he wanted to join him and Aryeh for lunch in the North End of Boston at this new Italian bistro he'd been meaning to try. Aaron said he'd take the T up to Haymarket and meet them since he wanted to run some quick errands on the way.

A gorgeous January Saturday in Boston, cold but not uncomfortable, Aaron met Jason and Aryeh at Rudolfo's Bistro. This time, Aryeh didn't shy away from him, but he wasn't exactly eager to be outgoing either. Seated by the window on strangely comfortable wrought iron chairs, all three slowly got to know one another—in truth, Aryeh wanted to see who this Aaron guy was that his father had told him about. Even at three, he was aware of everything around him, and he would certainly make it known to the entire restaurant if he weren't happy. Just after they ordered, Aaron mentioned that he brought a late Hanukkah gift for someone at the table. Jason shot him a "you didn't have to do that" look.

"Now, your dad mentioned to me that you liked lions, Aryeh, so I thought you might like this."

Out of the shopping bag came a stuffed golden lion with fluffy mane and all, and Aaron extended it to the youngest at the table. Aryeh looked at his father, who nodded, and then took the gift, putting his hands all over the mane and tail.

"What do you say?" Jason prompted.

"Thanks," Aryeh said, not even looking up. Aaron knew he'd done well.

Throughout the entire meal, Aryeh kept a watchful eye on his lion, seated carefully on the chair next to him, a cloth napkin haphazardly tied around the lion's neck. For every bite Jason's son took, he offered a bit to the lion, thinking that simply touching the mouth of the animal was enough to feed him. Thankfully, Aryeh only really ate bread, so the lion's fur was safe.

"Dare I ask how things went after I left your mom's house?" Aaron asked.

"China patterns and honeymoon arrangements," Jason said.

Aaron's eyes widened.

"Kidding! Seriously, though, you were a hit. I think my sisters want you to go out with them sometime to help them rate men. It might not be a bad idea."

"Your mom was very sweet to me, too. And your step-dad wanted to know everything I knew about teaching."

Jason sipped his iced tea. "You know, I may have been kidding about china patterns, but they really liked you, Aaron. You're the first guy I've brought to meet my parents who didn't go running after that experience."

"Someday, when you meet my parents, I'm afraid you'll be the one to go running."

"You've mentioned things are a little rough with your dad. But, we're just getting to know each other, so there's no rush on anything. I mean, I do want to meet your family..."

"I understand," Aaron said, smiling. "At some point in the future, we'll find some neutral territory and have a family gathering."

Aryeh wanted to get down from his chair and play with the lion, but Jason wanted him to stay near the table. He kissed his son's head as he lowered him to the floor. Every so often, Aaron looked to see where Aryeh was—Jason noticed. Lunch went by way too quickly, but Aryeh had to get back to Jason's parents house since Jason had a meeting at work he couldn't get out of. At first, Aaron almost suggested that he could watch Aryeh and just bring him by the Blumenfelds' later, but he wasn't entirely sure that Aryeh would be okay with that. Just because he liked the lion didn't mean he would like the one who gave it to him.

Jason and Aryeh walked Aaron back to the Haymarket station where Jason gave Aaron a tight hug and a peck on the cheek.

"Thank you," he said. "I'll call you after my meeting."

Aryeh put out his hand to shake Aaron's, the firmest handshake a three year old could give.

"Did you know that *aryeh* means lion in Hebrew?" Aryeh said.

Aaron squatted down a little. "Actually, I did know that. Why do you think I got it for you?" Aaron said, smiling. He had been doing that a lot, it seemed.

"Okay, little guy, let's go to grandma's house." Jason picked him up. "I might be available later for dinner, if you're free."

"Possibly. Just call or text me."

Just before they were too far apart, from a little mouth came, "Bye, Aaron!"

Progress, Aaron thought.

• • •

"More brisket?"

"Eh?" Aaron said.

"Do you want more brisket?" Adele asked, holding the platter. "We thought we lost you there."

"Sorry. Lost in thought for a moment. No, I'm good. Thanks, Mom."

Dinner only lasted about another thirty minutes before Adele kicked everyone out so she could put on coffee and get dessert ready. With a meat meal, they'd have to wait an hour before they could have dessert: cookies and homemade cheesecake. Aaron enjoyed that his parents still kept kosher after all these years. Jack was in his den, watching the news, when Aaron tapped on the doorframe.

"You busy?"

"Can you believe this guy? It's not bad enough that Congress can't get its collective head out from its own ass, but now they're promoting merit pay for teachers? Doesn't this just make you crazy?" Jack said, pointing at the screen.

"Yeah, I know. It's pretty ridiculous," Aaron said, sitting on the wing chair next to his father. "Now they're using the whole school's test scores to decide how each teacher does. Even when we haven't taught those kids."

"And you still want to teach, don't you. Regardless of all the *meshuginahs* in politics. I tell you... you should strike and see what happens."

"Heh. Dad, I'd probably lose my job. I'll call the senators and local reps, don't worry."

They watched the news for a few more minutes, and then Jack broke the silence.

"So, uh, your mother tells me you've met someone." He continued to look at the screen, even during the commercial.

Aaron sat there with nothing to say at first, just staring at the man in the recliner.

"Okay. Who are you and what have you done with my father?" he asked, trying to keep it light.

Jack let out a little chuckle. "Is he a good guy?"

"Dad. Seriously. What's going on? You've never asked about..."

"Look," Jack said, "your mother's been talking for months now about him... Jason, is it?"

"Okay, look..." He felt something wasn't right.

"Aaron, I'm fine. I just figured I'd ask."

He didn't expect to have a reaction, but Aaron got silent, fighting back tears. Was he happy his father asked? Was he just shocked that after all this time, he cared to ask? He tried to open his mouth, but no words came out. Then, his father turned off the television.

Jack sighed and brought the recliner back upright.

"I want you to understand something, so just listen. No, I'm not sick or dying. If there's anything I have, it's blindness, for you. You're my only son, Aaron, and I've always wanted better for you than I had. Growing up in Dorchester wasn't easy, trust me. If a guy even wore certain types of after-shave, his friends gave him a hard time. I watched guys have the crap kicked out of them all the time if people even thought they were... faygeleh. People I was good friends with in college used to talk about how many 'queers' they found in back alleys in downtown Boston, having sex or Lord knows what—I wasn't there, so I don't know. But, what I do know is that I didn't want that to happen to *my* son. It's not easy, Aaron, being from a blue-collar family, raised by a single father. Papa Sam taught your Uncle Morris and me how to defend ourselves and how to work hard at something, so I did. When you were born, I promised your mother I would teach you right from wrong, how to stand up and be a man, and most importantly, have self-respect. I did my best."

Caught up in the moment, Aaron took a few breaths before he spoke.

"Dad, when I tried to stand up and 'be a man', taking responsibility for myself, you all but shunned me. I agonized for months about coming out to you and Mom, fearing I'd be kicked out of the house and disowned. Your constant questions whether I had met any young women or whether I was ever interested in getting married grated on me for a long time. It made me regret being honest to you. I should have just lied about it all, told you what you wanted to hear, just so you would stop looking at me with disappointment."

Like his son, Jack also didn't know quite how to respond, but Aaron wasn't quite finished, either.

"So, what changed, Dad? Why all of a sudden this interest in my social life? We've always been able to talk or argue politics, my job, even sports when the Red Sox play. I'm just curious to know what's different now."

"I guess I don't want to lose my son, my only son. You haven't been here in months. For a while, we'd all have Shabbos dinner together and then play cards all night. Last summer, actually, was the last time we did that because you were always so busy during the year. After that, I saw you on Rosh Hashanah at your Aunt Pesha's." He took a moment. "I'm not very good with talking about my feelings, Aaron. The people I talk to, men from my generation, aren't as enlightened as I am, let me tell you. Some of these guys are real conservatives with beliefs about putting prayer back in schools, so that kids—your kids— won't have a choice. None of this 'moment of silence'. It'll be 'prayer time', and kids will be harassed because they're either a different faith or no faith. I've never believed in that. Prayer's good for synagogues, churches, mosques, wherever. Anyway, my point is, I'm one of the more enlightened guys in this neighborhood. Looking back on all the stuff I've seen and the people I've known, I started paying more attention to issues. Now, I'm not saying I'll march in any parades or join PFLAG, but I decided it was either I change a little... or I lose my son."

Jack stood up from the chair and patted Aaron on the shoulder before walking out of the room. That would be his way of saying he loved his son. A few minutes later, after he pulled himself together, Aaron joined the family in the living room while his mother put the rest of the dessert and coffee out. Rachel jumped off the couch and took her brother by the hand.

"Come sit with me. You okay? We heard you and Dad talking, and it seemed to get a little intense."

Aaron nodded, kissing her on the top of her head. "It's good."

The Feldman family had dispensed long ago with cards and gifts for Mother's and Father's Day, and instead just had dinner or brunch together. Both Jack and Sally felt cards were wasteful and preferred calls or emails. It worked out better anyway, since the family gatherings were much more interesting. Every once in a while, Aaron would catch his father looking at him, and it would make him smile. Jack smiled back. No words needed.

At 9:00 p.m., the doorbell rang, but everyone was busy playing cards, so Aaron answered the door.

"Jason? Wow. What are you doing here? And Aryeh's with you..."

"I was invited. You going to let me in?" he said, laughing.

"Of course! Come in. I'm sorry. I just wasn't expecting you." He hugged Jason a little tighter than usual and kissed him quickly.

"That's why they call it a surprise."

"Well, um, come on in. Hey, Aryeh. How's it going, buddy?" He held out his hand for a high five, and Aryeh complied.

As they walked into the living room, Rachel saw them first and jumped up from the card table.

"Yay! I'm glad you could make it," she said to Jason. "And this must be Aryeh. Come on in, and let me introduce you."

Sally and Aaron watched as Jason introduced himself to Robert and then Jack, who stood up and shook Jason's hand. Aaron felt almost apoplectic, but he decided to go with the moment. Rachel took Aryeh by the hand and asked if he wanted a black and white cookie. She took his hopping up and down as an affirmative and guided him toward the dining room table.

"Mom, why didn't you tell me you were going to invite Jason?" he said, his arm around her shoulders.

"Well, it would have ruined the surprise, and besides, I'm not the one who invited him."

"I'm going to kill Rachel," he laughed. "She's always poking—"

"Not Rachel, either."

"Dad?"

Sally nodded. "Don't ask me when, but one day last week I noticed that your number wasn't on the refrigerator where I always keep it. When I asked your father, he told me what he'd done. I couldn't ruin the surprise, Aaron. It would have broken his heart. He really has tried to change. And, he was a perfect gentleman on the phone, too."

"I'm sure he was." Aaron couldn't handle any more surprises.

Now it was Jason's turn for the inquisition, but he didn't mind. And the one asking the most questions was Jack. After all, if some man was in his son's life, he had to know that this man was going to take good care of his son. Aaron watched Rachel play with Aryeh—that little boy had opened up so much since they'd met in January. Aryeh's toy bag sat in the hallway, and Aaron saw a golden, furry figure poking out the top. He still had the lion. Every few questions, someone would ask Aaron something, so he felt obliged to stay near the conversation while also keeping an eye on the three year old who had stolen his heart. Whenever the boy wanted Jason's attention, he called for his *Aba*, Hebrew for 'Daddy', and Aaron felt such a warmth, as if he had been blessed with two such wondrous people. Rachel let Aaron have a few moments to play with Aryeh, and now it was Jason's turn to feel blessed. He had always wanted someone in his life who could share his love for his son. It was still too soon, but he felt that in the not too distant future, he wanted to make his relationship with Aaron more permanent—much more.

As it got closer to 10:30, Jason wanted to get Aryeh back home so he started making his goodbyes to the Feldman family. Rachel and Robert wanted to get dinner with the guys sometime during the week, but that depended on Jason's schedule mostly. While the adults were chatting a bit longer, Aryeh retrieved the lion and an envelope, bringing both back into the living room.

"Before we go," Jason started, "I wanted to say something to Aaron, but I want you all to hear it. He's not only very special to me, but he's also become a big part of Aryeh's life, too. When we first met, I know my little guy was shy, but over the months, Aryeh and Aaron have warmed up to one another. He wanted to make you a card, Aaron, but he asked my parents to help him write it. The words were his, so it's as much of a surprise to me as it will be to you. Go ahead, Aryeh. Give it to him."

Aaron knelt down to Aryeh's level and opened the card. A few seconds into reading it, tears flowed from Aaron's face, tears like he hadn't shed before. He handed the card to Jason, who read it aloud:

"Aba Aaron, I hope you stay forever. Love, Aryeh (it means lion)"

Aaron looked up and saw his father had stepped back into the living room, so he went to him.

"You okay, Dad?"

Jack, standing by the sliding glass doors to the backyard, had his eyes closed and rocked a little.

"Dad?"

His father nodded slightly. "I'm sorry, Aaron."

"For what?"

"For not being a better father."

Aaron turned his father to face him. "Dad, you know something, I have always loved you, but I have never been prouder that you're my father than right now."

Both men embraced, the kind that should have happened a long time ago, and then Jason stepped into the living room.

"Aaron, I have to get going."

Jack waved him over to them. "It was a pleasure getting to know you, Jason. As far as I'm concerned, you're a real mensch, and you should be as proud of your son as I am of mine." And then he hugged Jason.

"Mr. Feldman, you have my word that I'll take the best care of Aaron. I promise."

Jack patted the two men on the back and went into his den. Once all the goodbyes had finished, Aaron, Jason, and Aryeh headed to their respective cars. Just before Aaron got into his, Jason told him to come over later after Aryeh was asleep.

"Oh, and Aaron? Happy Father's Day."

JULY

FOURTH OF JULY:
"THE SAD (AND ALMOST TRUE) STORY OF JIMMY THE HUSTLER"
BY MITCHUM SINCLAIR

Today was the day. Jimmy was getting out of hooking. He'd been thinking about it for a few weeks, but hadn't acted on it yet. Independence Day was the best time to make a clean break. The symbolism was just too good to pass up (besides, he could make some good money between now and then to pay the bills until he got an honest job).

Jimmy had been hooking in Austin since he was 15. He had a rare beauty that was apparent to everyone around him, especially his step father. Zach never touched Jimmy, but he saw the potential for money and began to pimp Jimmy out while Jimmy's mother was out of the house. Jimmy never knew how Zach built up such a client list, but he was kept busy. At first, it was the dregs of society, unfit, ugly men with uglier wives who just needed a blowjob, and they didn't care how they got it. As the client list got longer, the clientele became a bit nicer. Clean cut college-educated and closeted. These men had some money to spare and would occasionally bring Jimmy jewelry (or one time, an Xbox 360 with 10 games!). The family began to become flush with money. They moved into a real house (one without wheels) and started buying stuff. If Jimmy's mother ever wondered where all the money was coming from, she never asked. After about 2 years of this, Jimmy began to realize he was the breadwinner in the family, and really had all the power. He realized he had other muscles to flex and the balance of power began to shift.

'Not taking any clients this weekend, Zach, I'm going to Lake Travis.'

'The fuck you are! I've got you booked for the next month. Besides, we need the cash. I just bought a new truck.'

'Re-schedule, Zach. They'll come around. I'm worth it.'

Zach would often threaten to beat Jimmy up, but they both knew it was an empty threat. A battered and bruised Jimmy was no good to anyone. Jimmy's clientele preferred pretty boys, without blemish.

Jimmy packed his bags for the weekend and took off. There was a Beer and Bong party at a lake house. He got the invitation from a client. He accepted with the pre-requisite that this was not a working party. If Jimmy had any sex this weekend, it would be for fun, and he would get to pick the lucky guy.

The lake house was awash with lights when Jimmy pulled into the drive. Cars were everywhere, and every square inch of the balconies were crowded with bodies. A quick check in the rearview mirror to make sure his blonde locks were tidy and attractive and Jimmy bounded into the place like he owned it. Everyone he passed tried to get his attention, but Jimmy was headed for the bar. A stiff drink was required before he could settle in and socialize. As he made his way across the crowded living room, Jimmy's keen eye spotted at least 5 other hustlers. From their body language and proximity to their conversation partner, Jimmy could tell they were all working. Jimmy was reminded how well he really had it, as far as hooking went. No longer living hand to mouth, he could afford not to work for a few days. As he approached the bar, he felt a hand from behind, clasp his shoulder.

'Jimmy! So glad you could make it. I was beginning to wonder,' Alan, the host was a nice guy and a good client, but he tended to dress and act like he was still in his 30s instead of the more appropriate clothes a 72 year old should be wearing. He handed Jimmy a joint.

Jimmy took a long drag before answering. 'Of course I would come, Alan! My favorite client, booze, and the best weed. How could I turn you down?' He took another hit before handing it back.

'Listen, I know you aren't working, but I have some business associates from out of town, and they'd love to meet you, if only to set up something for later in the week. Whaddaya say?'

'No business tonight, Alan. Give them my card. But hey, if I happened to be introduced to them later, no harm, right?' He winked at Alan as he turned back to the bar.

Several hours, 2 beers, countless hits off the bong and too many shots to count, Alan walked up to Jimmy. He was accompanied by 2 men of indeterminate age, Jimmy would have guessed 45, but their appearance had an ageless quality to it. Maybe it was just the buzz.

'Jimmy, may I introduce Kyle and Hal. Brothers visiting from the Portland area. Kyle, Hal, this is Jimmy, the young man I've been telling you about.'

'It's a pleasure to meet you Jimmy,' said Hal, 'We've heard a lot about you from Alan. He's been very pleased with you and how you operate your business. I can see now how you attract so many first rate clients.'

'Thanks, man, but I'm not here to talk business. This is a party and I'm just here to enjoy myself. Alan can get you my number and you can set something up through my manager for later in the week. I'm totally ok with brothers. I have a nice little act for that. Which one of you wants to be my best friend and which one wants to walk in on us?'

Hal and Kyle laughed. 'Oh dear, there seems to be a misconception. We're not here to sample the goods, dear boy. We're here to recruit you for business.' Kyle explained.

Jimmy stared at them blankly, the drugs doing their best to delay comprehension. 'Uh dude, I'm only in one kind of business, and I do fine on my own.'

Hal looked at Jimmy, 'Do you? From what Alan tells us, your step father is your 'manager' and he keeps you pretty busy with clients of his choosing. You think you have a lot of money, but do you know how much he's keeping for himself?'

Kyle continued, 'We run a VERY selective escort service in the Pacific Northwest. Only the cream of the crop. We have a rigorous selection process for clients and an even more rigorous and discreet process for selecting our employees. We'd set you up in a nice penthouse, no roommates. Nice wardrobe, nice ride. Answering service. Everything a young man like you could possibly need. All we ask is 10% of your earnings and a 10 year exclusive contract with us.'

'10%??!! How do you know how much I am going to charge?'

'Oh, we'll do all your bookings through our agency. You are forbidden from taking side jobs, or boyfriends for that matter,' Hal explained.

'If the selection process is underway, I can do you right now. Let's go to the bedroom.'

Again, laughter.

'Jimmy, you've been auditioning with me the whole time,' Alan explained, 'I'm what you might call a Talent Scout.'

'I guess this means he's interested,' Hal said to Kyle.

'Fuck yeah! When do we leave?'

'That's entirely up to you. We're leaving in the morning, but if you need to tie up some loose ends, we'll send the jet for you at the end of the week,' Kyle offered.

'Screw that. There's nothing here I need to tie up. Let's get the fuck out of here.'

'Well, there is the matter of the contract. We'll need it signed before we leave. I want to make sure every 'i' is dotted and every 't' is crossed.' Hal was the one with the business sense. He opened the portfolio in his hand and pulled out a manila envelope with several official looking documents. All of them had Jimmy's name (his real name) pre-printed. Jimmy scanned them and looked up at Hal and Kyle.

'How did you know I would say yes, and how do you know my name?'

Kyle and Hal looked at each other, 'We do our homework,' Kyle said cryptically.

12 hours later, Jimmy was ensconced in his new penthouse, a brand new employee of the Occidental Agency. The brothers owned a sumptuous building downtown emblazoned with the initials OA on it, as a cover. The building housed not only the penthouses for the dozen or so escorts, but several legitimate businesses as well: Accounting firm, Temp Agency, Communications company, anything legitimate which they could also recruit employees for the Agency. Jimmy had no idea how many receptionists, accountants, CPAs, and phone operators it took to run a high end service like this. All Jimmy had to do was show up at the appointed time and place and do his stuff.

By the time he was 4 years into his contract, Jimmy's 'stuff' became more elaborate. Gone were the days of just showing up. There were characters to create, costumes to wear (albeit briefly), and techniques to master. Not to mention these high end clients tended to look like Moby Dick. To a man, they were all old, overweight and not concerned at all with actively participating in each event. Jimmy often wondered why his right arm wasn't significantly bigger than his left, considering how many appointments ended with hand jobs.

It was when Guy showed up that things really started going downhill. By this time, Jimmy had become the star of the outfit, and as such, had a very full schedule. The car, the clothes and the penthouse didn't really do much for him, since he was never home. Every damned day was booked solid. It was a wonder they even accepted a new client for him, repeat business was really all he could keep up with.

Guy opened the door, wearing a leather jacket (no shirt), black denim pants (commando) and leather boots. Jimmy could instantly tell he was an asshole, the costume was just extra.

'Hi, I'm Jim-'

'Shut the fuck up and get naked!'

Ok, it was role play from the beginning. It's not the first time. Jimmy could hang. He got undressed and stood there, waiting for instructions.

Guy walked around him slowly, examining the product. Jimmy could hear his rattled breath. He was definitely a smoker. Jimmy hated that, but again, he could cope. It's all part of the job. Guy stopped directly behind Jimmy, his hot breath wheezed on Jimmy's neck.

'You look nice, boy, but what the Hell makes you think you're so special?'

Jimmy knew immediately the part he was supposed to play, 'I'm not special, sir, I'm just here to please you.'

The force of Guy's punch knocked the breath out of Jimmy and sent him across the room. He landed with a thud against the sofa.

'Don't give me that rent boy script! I'm not playing a game with you. I paid a lot of fucking money to get you here and you are gonna talk to me like a human being!' Guy snarled.

'Listen asshole, I'm here to do a job, whatever you like. but if you want me off script, and you want a real conversation, fucking talk to me. Otherwise I suggest you get back to Daddy Drill Sergeant and let's get this over with.'

'Fine, crawl over here and lick my fucking boot, junior.'

Jimmy hated Guy. He'd been in leather situations before, but Guy was different. Guy never got off, and almost never took off his clothes. He was content to get Jimmy naked, humiliate him, and on occasion watch Jimmy jack off. When they were done, Guy would shove Jimmy naked into the hallway and throw his clothes after him. More than once, Guy's neighbors had caught him getting dressed.

After the third or fourth session, Jimmy went to see Hal and Kyle. He wanted Guy off his roster.

'I'm so sorry, Jimmy, but Guy pays a premium to have you service him,' Hal explained.

'A fucking premium? How much? Why don't I see a penny of that?'

'It's in the contract, Jimmy. We keep the premiums we charge to clients. It pays for the added expense of setting everything up. That's not Guy's apartment for one, we own that.'

'I don't want to see Guy. It's that simple. It's also in my contract that I get to approve my clients. I remember that. Do you?'

Hal and Kyle looked at each other.

'Well, it's not that simple. You see here, in the fine print, we can override you when it comes to premium clients like Guy,' Hal was very good at sounding sincerely unhappy when pointing out information that benefitted him and not Jimmy.

'WHAT THE FUCK???!!!' Jimmy snatched the contract out of Hal's hands and scanned it quickly. Seeing the offensive fine print, he threw it back in Hal's face. His blood was boiling, he was furious, but smart enough to know this was his own damned fault. He just sat there and stewed.

'We know you're upset, but what is one irritating client next to the hundreds of others that are more appealing? Think of the nice things a couple of hours with Guy can buy you?' Kyle tried to reassure Jimmy.

'More appealing?' Jimmy huffed derisively.

'You seem a little on edge, my boy. Why not take a couple of weeks off? I have a lovely suite at the Palazzo Sasso on the Amalfi Coast. Take the jet and go there to clear your head for a while. We'll clear your schedule and you can recharge your batteries, so to speak,' Hal offered.

It did sound like a nice idea, but Jimmy was still too pissed to see anything clearly. He didn't want their charity, he didn't want their rules, and for the first time, he thought about just chucking it all and giving up on the lifestyle.

'No thanks. I'd rather just buy out my contract. I think I'm done with you boys.'

'Oh dear, I'm so sorry you feel that way, Jimmy, but there's no buyout option. You still owe us 3 years of service, non-negotiable,' Hal was a pro at this.

Jimmy grabbed his stuff and bolted for the door. As he walked up to his penthouse, it really sank in. Jimmy was deluding himself that he was his own man, that he was master of his destiny. When he left Austin a lifetime ago, he congratulated himself on the strength of his will. HE made the decision, and he was reaping the benefits. It was only now that he realized the OA brothers were his puppet masters, so skillfully manipulating him and everything around him that he never noticed. Well, that was gonna stop, right now. Only, he didn't know how. The only thing he ever knew was hustling. What else could he possibly do? In this world, he was a Star, he was Somebody. What was he outside of this? Just another runaway with no family, no friends, and no real prospects. He sat down on the edge of his enormous bed nearly sliding off the satin emerald green comforter. Staring out over his bedroom, looking at all of his things, Jimmy realized that deep down, he didn't want to quit. He just wanted to have things his way. If he was going to stay (and it looked increasingly like he had no choice), he was at least going to get a free vacation out of it. He grabbed his phone and dialed.

'Listen, sorry about that tantrum, Kyle. I know, I'm just a little tired. Is that vacation offer still on the table? Great. I'll go ahead and wrap up this week's appointments, it's the least I can do. But Sunday I want to be in the air, on my way to Italy.'

He felt better already.

Settling in to his luxurious room at the Palazzo Sasso, Jimmy looked out over the ocean, inhaling a deep breath of the salt sea air. The flight had been uneventful, Jimmy slept most of the way, and there was nothing to unpack. Jimmy had decided this trip would require an entirely new wardrobe, one he could procure here on the Amalfi Coast. Instead, he uncorked the champagne management had presented to him, and sipped it out of a crystal flute as he looked out at the sunset. The room almost glowed, the sunlight reflecting off the cream colored ivory walls, and the soft yellow of the curtains. Jimmy felt more alive, more real than he ever did working. It was a beautiful feeling, and it revitalized him. No jet lag here, Jimmy gulped down his champagne and walked out of the hotel. It was the perfect opportunity for an evening stroll.

Walking down the cobbled streets of Ravello, Jimmy saw mom and pop shops of every kind: bakeries, jewelry, clothiers, and old bookshops. He fought the urge to stop in every single one of them. He was going to be here for a while, he needed to pace himself. He had all the time in the world to explore this little slice of heaven.

It was then that he saw something lurking in an alley. Curiosity getting the better of him, Jimmy backed up and peered down the dark corridor. There, partially covered in shadow, was a young man. He was leaning against the brick wall, smoking a cigarette. Brown locks of hair fell over his eyes, covering his face, with the exception of full, plump lips. He put the cigarette between those lips and inhaled slowly and deeply. As he exhaled, Jimmy's gaze went south, to the tight clingy striped shirt, hugging every crevasse of his torso. A thick, white belt held up beautiful white bell bottoms which were as tight as the shirt, and hid nothing. One leg was drawn up on the wall. The look was very nautical and seductive. The young man looked at Jimmy, took another long drag, and spoke.

'American? Cigarette?'

Jimmy couldn't move, but simply said, 'No thanks, I don't smoke.'

Sailor boy dropped his cigarette to the ground, and stamped it out with his black Prada slip ons. He walked to Jimmy.

'Good time, I show you. Good deal I make you.'

This boy was trying to hustle Jimmy. He laughed out loud before he could help himself. The boy was so caught off guard and hurt, he spun on his heels to walk away.

'No, don't!' Jimmy shouted, 'I'm sorry, I'm not laughing at you. I'm just happy to see you,' Jimmy could be a quick thinker when the need arose.

Sailor boy stopped. He turned around and looked straight into Jimmy's eyes. 'Don't laugh at me. I am a good boy, I make you happy.'

'I'm sure you can. But let's start this over. My name is Jimmy. I'm on vacation here for a while. Yes, I am American. No, I'm not looking for a good time. I am looking for a friend. Would you like to accompany me to dinner?'

Sailor boy looked at Jimmy. He could see the gears turning is his head as he tried to decide if he could afford to lose time to make money by eating.

'Look, if it will help you make up your mind, I'll pay you for your time. Whatever your rate is, double it. Just don't think you're gonna be putting out later tonight.'

Sailor boy smiled, 'My name is Stefan. I would be happy to join you for dinner.' So, his English was actually better when he wasn't trying to hustle. Jimmy found that cute.

They returned to the hotel and dined at the in-house restaurant. Stefan in his mostly white sailor garb looked at home in the black and white decor. He ate modestly, but earnestly, and entertained Jimmy with stories of Italy, his friends, and of books. Stefan was an avid reader, mostly of popular American fiction. He imagined America to be one big country full of heroic lawyers, crime solving detectives, sparkly vampires and Chelsea Handler. Jimmy was expecting to see Italy through the eyes of this native, and instead, was presented a version of his country seen through the lens of Stefan. He tried to correct some of the misconceptions Stefan had, but eventually gave up. Partly because there were too many, and partly because he began to feel like a parent telling his kid that Santa Claus isn't real.

As dinner wound down, and the champagne bottles piled up, Jimmy realized he was feeling something entirely new, something he had forgotten how to feel: Genuine attraction to another man. Stefan was not a client, he was not just another body. They were getting along so well, it felt like a real date (or what Jimmy assumed a real date was. Had he ever really had one?) He dreaded saying good night to Stefan, but he knew it was inevitable. Not only did Stefan need to go make some more money, but Jimmy didn't know how to act in bed if it wasn't a job. He wondered how Stefan felt, after all he was being paid to be there. At that moment, Stefan leaned over and kissed Jimmy, deeply.

'That was free,' was all he said. He stood up and walked out of the hotel, leaving Jimmy sitting there, watching him walk out. He didn't even ask Jimmy to pay him.

Jimmy woke up the next morning unable to get the thought of Stefan out of his head. As he sipped coffee on his balcony, he reconstructed the entire night from memory, and tried to decide what to do next. If Stefan was working again, he probably would not be out again until tonight. Would he be in the same place? Would he have a client? Did he even want to see Jimmy again? Not ever really having dated, Jimmy knew he was becoming a little obsessive a little too quickly. He needed a distraction. He dressed and went back into the village for a little retail therapy. New clothes always made Jimmy feel better.

4 hours later, Jimmy walked back into the hotel, dapper new linen suit, leather messenger bag, and new Prada shoes. He'd also taken in a visit to a local barber to get a shave and a haircut. He was the picture of refinement and swagger. The rest of his shopping would be delivered to the hotel directly, which was a good thing. If he'd had any bags with them he would have dropped them at the sight of Stefan sitting in the lobby waiting for him.

'I thought you might want to go sightseeing with me.'

Jimmy was so excited at the prospect of spending more time with Stefan, he ran up to him, grabbed his hand, and pulled him out the doors back into the village.

Jimmy and Stefan spent the next two weeks together. Everyday, Stefan would meet him downstairs for breakfast, and then they would pick something to do and go out into the city. The day would finish back at the hotel for dinner, but Stefan never stayed over. Jimmy didn't bring it up, because frankly, he was afraid of how sex would work in a relationship. Yes, Jimmy admitted, he was dating Stefan. It was exciting, thrilling, scary, and most of all, it made Jimmy happy.

Jimmy's last day in Italy was a somber one for Stefan. As they sailed around the coast in a rented boat, Jimmy drank mimosas and kept grinning mischievously at Stefan. Assuming Jimmy was excited about going home, it made Stefan's mood even darker. As the sun set over the water, Stefan looked at Jimmy.

'It is time for me to go back. Thank you for the lovely time.'

'No, no, Stefan. I have a surprise for you, stay a little while longer, please.'

'No, you leave tomorrow, and I do not want to spend another minute here, it will hurt too much.'

'Just wait here a sec,' Jimmy went down to the hold and brought up a basket. and a bottle of wine, 'I packed us a dinner for the boat. Please, eat with me and then we'll go back.'

Stefan capitulated as they dined on cold pasta and salad whipped up by the hotel chef. They drained the bottle of wine quickly. Jimmy was smart enough to bring several more.

'Listen, I'm leaving tomorrow, that's true, but that doesn't mean it's the end for us. Come back with me. I think I want to make a life with you, Stefan. We can both leave the hustling behind. I don't know what we'll do, but I've got some money to my name and we can live on that while we figure out what to do, together. Come with me, please.'

Stefan looked over at Jimmy, tears streaming down his face, 'I love you, Jimmy. I would make a life with you. I never thought I would be able to leave this life, and here you are, giving me a way out,' he pulled Jimmy close, and kissed him, wrapping his arms around Jimmy, holding him tight.

'Let's spend the night on the boat.'

Jimmy's plan was simple, fly back to Portland on the OA jet, and let Stefan fly back commercial a week later, so as not to alert the brothers. Jimmy would resume his schedule, to get some extra cash, and quietly move some things out of the penthouse to a hotel where he would put Stefan up. After that they would both leave Portland for somewhere on the east coast. Stefan voted for New York, but Jimmy knew that would be too obvious. Philadelphia was better. Jimmy's friends Anthony and Nick could house them for a few days as they began a new life. He attacked his clients with renewed gusto, telling himself it didn't matter, in a week he'd be gone.

Jimmy woke up on July 4th, feeling better than he'd ever felt. He was going to fit in a few clients before lunch, pick Stefan up at the airport, and watch the city fireworks from the penthouse one last time before they started their new life. After a quick shower, Jimmy checked his schedule. Crap, his last appointment of the day was with Guy. Fuck it, he could deal with Guy's shit one more time.

Jimmy tried to catch his breath. That last punch had really knocked the wind out of him. Guy was in rare form today. His punches seemed a lot harder, the pre-strip beating seemed longer.

'Get up.'

Jimmy crawled up the wall to maintain his balance. All the while he was smiling. Go on, you bastard, give me all you got. I'll never see your fucking face again.

'That's a good boy. Worn out? We got a lot more to do. Take off your shirt.'

Jimmy gently peeled off the tee, he could see the beginnings of a bruise under his left nipple. That was gonna stay for a while. He grinned as he thought of Stefan caressing it.

'What are you smiling at? Do you think this is fun??? Take off those pants.'

Jimmy stifled his grin as he unbuttoned his pants slowly, just like Guy wanted it. Now that he was naked, Guy sat down in his chair.

'You know what comes next. My boots are dirty, clean them up.'

Jimmy crawled across the floor and began to lick the dirt off of Guy's boots. They were extra dirty today, but still, Jimmy couldn't keep from smiling. His thoughts drifted to Stefan again.

'I ain't gonna tell you again, wipe that fucking grin off your goddamned face!'

Jimmy felt a crack as Guy's boot connected with his breast bone, hard. He fell back, grasping his chest, trying to catch his breath.

'See what you did? This is my show boy, and you do as I tell you to!'

Another kick, this one to the spleen. Jimmy tried to scream, but his breath was still caught in his chest.

'Get the fuck up!' Guy grabbed Jimmy by the hair and dragged him up to a standing position. Jimmy's eyes were wild.

'Please, …stop. Something's wrong,' he whispered.

'Aw, Boo Fuckin' Hoo. Don't try to weasel out of this. You know how this goes. Take it like a man!' Guy threw Jimmy face first into the coffee table. The glass top shattered on contact. Jimmy collapsed.

'Get up.'

'Get Up!'

'I'm FUCKING serious. Get the FUCK UP!'

'Oh Jesus. Oh God. Oh FUCK!'

'Hello? Kyle? Something happened to Jimmy. It was an accident. Get someone over here, fast. I can't be seen here. Yeah, usual room. No, I won't touch anything.'

Stefan waited at the Portland airport for 4 hours before he decided to try and find Jimmy on his own. Jimmy had given Stefan a key and directions to the penthouse in case his appointments ran long. As the elevator doors opened up, Stefan saw a crowd of men coming in and out of Jimmy's penthouse. It looked like they were moving things. He cautiously stepped inside. Movers were packing up furniture, clothes, everything. Maybe Jimmy had come clean to his bosses. Maybe they didn't have to run.

'I'm sorry this is a private residence. Can I help you?' said a man of indeterminate age.

'Oh I, uh, I'm sorry, I was looking for a friend. Hi- His name is Jimmy.'

'Dear boy, I am afraid Jimmy is no longer with us. He, well, he went on to bigger and better things.'

'He left me?'

'I'm afraid so. He didn't say anything to anyone. I think perhaps he found something better to move on to. I'm so sorry, I didn't catch you name.'

'Stefan.'

'Well, Stefan, you look hungry, and tired. Why don't I take you somewhere to eat, and maybe I can help you find someplace to stay, perhaps even a job, if you're looking. My name is Kyle.'

Charlie finished reading the final draft. It was good to finally have Jimmy excised from his brain. Jimmy was done, and so was the story. He'd fly to New York tonight and deliver it to Random House in the morning, after a download, of course...

AUGUST / SEPTEMBER

BIRTHDAY:
"FIFTY"
BY HANK HENDERSON

It didn't help when the AARP membership arrived exactly one day before my birthday. The envelope was delivered so exactly on time that I stood at the mailbox and imagined a nondescript van parked across the street from my house. It would've been the kind used for wiretapping in spy movies: somber, windowless, perhaps with a fake company name and address stenciled on the door panel. Inside there would have been a team of spinsters with their hair up in buns as tight as their smiles, all of them diligently leafing through yearbooks and peering through peepholes.

"Did he see the envelope?"

"It's in his hands now."

"Then rev it up, Hattie. There are six more to verify today between here and Pasadena."

For several weeks I had been telling anyone who asked, anyone who would listen, anyone within earshot that if anything, all I wanted for my birthday was dinner or a movie. No big party. No mob of people I don't particularly regard as friends forcing congratulations on me while drinking my liquor. No, really, no party, especially no surprise party. And most of all, nobody sings that goddamn song. I'm turning fifty. So what? All I really wanted for my birthday was nothing at all. That's what.

Of course Mom called. She told me she was going to send a single black balloon as a joke but couldn't find a florist that had one.

"Probably because of Halloween," she said, as if people send each other bouquets of black balloons as Halloween gifts.

Still, I smiled at the thought of my mother nestled in her hunter green La-Z-Boy, the yellow pages in her lap, patiently calling florist to florist and explaining why she wanted them to deliver a single black balloon.

"Your sister says to tell you it's just a number and that it's no big deal," Mom said. Then she began to tell me about an article she read in *Good Housekeeping* about how to repurpose leftover Halloween candy into clever table decorations.

"Just in case you're having a party," she said.

While Mom went on I drifted off, thought how my sister is younger than me. It's always the teenager telling the 30-year-old it's no big deal. It's the 27-year-old with a full head of hair and no body fat saying that forty is just a number. My sister is not 27 and I'm not forty but she is younger and it is a big deal. It's fifty. The Big Five-Oh. Half a century for chrissakes. I wouldn't even be in advertiser's hallowed 18-49 demographic anymore. The future held nothing but AARP discount tickets, large print books and stretch Dockers. There was no reason to celebrate.

Mom finally asked, "So what are you doing for your birthday?"

"Nothing," I said, and snapped back into the conversation. "Well, friends are taking me to dinner the day after tomorrow. You remember Mark and Bryan? They know the owner of a restaurant next to the Santa Monica Pier.

The owners are going to comp our meal. We're going to have the kind of dinner we wish we really could afford. But it's not a birthday dinner, just a dinner around my birthday."

"Riiight," Mom said with a fake drawl that stretched halfway to Texas.

*　*　*

Getting ready to go out to dinner on Friday took less than an hour. Finding something to wear was less a fashion crisis and more a process of elimination. There was 'too summery' and there was 'too tight.' I pulled out my favorite black sweater. Not too bad. It's slimming, I think.

"It's so solemn," Joe said.

"It's not a party," I replied.

"It's your birthday."

A horn sounded in the driveway.

"It's time to go," I said.

*　*　*

When the four of us entered the Lobster, the maître d', tall, tan with black hair that fell across his forehead and stopped just above ocean blue eyes, greeted Mark and Bryan by name. The alcohol infused conversation drifted down from the bar at the top of the stairs and drowned out whatever Mark and the maître d' were talking about. With a quick toss of his hair, the maître d' leaned around Mark to include all four of us and suggested we wait in the bar until our table was ready.

The bar was filled with a wide variety of people who seemed to have one thing in common: they never looked at prices when ordering from menus. Leggy women wore tall shoes and short skirts. Men looked like they owned things large and expensive. Oversized chunky jewelry of mismatched metal shapes rested on purchased décolletage. Shirt cuffs landed exactly at the wrist. Facial stubble had artistic flair. Shoes were Italian, hair geometric, layered and dyed. Lips were plumped, tummies tucked, eyes done. Faces lifted with a practiced look of interest in whatever was going to be said next.

I stood at the end of the bar and did the 'adjust the sweater but secretly flick the finger to make sure my zipper's up' move on my three seasons ago Banana Republic slacks and tried my best not to feel my age.

When Mark leaned over and asked what I wanted to drink, I scanned the crowded room and said, "something strong without singing or candles."

Our round of drinks had barely arrived when the maître d' appeared. He tossed his head and hair flicked across his forehead in the direction of the table where we were going to be seated. We made our way through a crowd of people who had been waiting much longer than us and were taken to the best window seat in the house. The view stretched from Venice to the south up north to Point Dume in Malibu. We sat down in time to watch the day give way to a pink dusted, silvery dusk. Just outside the restaurant the Santa Monica pier was crazy alive with people and motion, from the Ferris wheel's ever-changing kaleidoscope of electric neon patterns to the whimsical blue and yellow striped Cirque du Soleil tent.

I settled into the easy camaraderie of dinner with my man and our longtime friends. We laughed and talked our way through Alaskan King crab, oysters, tiger shrimp, sashimi, wine, more cocktails...and that was just the appetizers. I relaxed and enjoyed myself even though I was not having a birthday. After our table had been cleared and drinks were empty our waiter came up behind me.

"I almost forgot this," he said as he set down tiramisu, blueberry cobbler and ice creams. The waiter put his hand on my shoulder and leaned down. "Happy non-birthday," he said and winked.

"How's that for subtle?" Bryan said.

After the meal, the four of us decided to walk along the parkway that overlooks the cliff. The Cirque show had begun; its music rode out of the big top on waves of applause and colored the parkway with a magical, festive air. I remembered the Hearst beach house had been renovated and just reopened on the beach. Not knowing it was well over a mile away, I suggested we go take a look at it. So, we crossed the pedestrian bridge over PCH to go investigate.

The circus music faded away behind us as we walked and talked our way down the quiet and empty bike path. The moon shone heavy and low over the ocean as if spent from having been full just days before.

Up ahead of us I noticed a group of about three dozen kids gathered at the curb between the parking lot and the bike path. Their music came to our ears slowly as if cued by the moon. When we meandered close enough to be noticed, a dreadlocked blonde girl on the tumbling edge of the bobbing mass of bodies waved her arms at us and yelled, "Come dance with us!"

Speaker Girl motioned to someone in the crowd and then turned and tinkered with two large decal covered speakers that sat on a rickshaw like add-on connected to a dusty mountain bike. The bike was one of a herd tired and waiting while their riders danced to a rowdy, funky Rasta remix. A boy, not tall, blond, hovering around nineteen, came out of the crowd as if by slingshot.

"Hi! We're dancing." He looked at us with a genuine curiosity. "What are you guys doing down here?"

Mark reached out and took the boy's shoulder and nonchalantly said, "It's our friend's birthday." I blanched as the word ricocheted through the dancing crowd.

Blond Nineteen glanced at each of us to the beat of the music and asked, "Whose birthday?" I tried to blend into the darkness beyond the glow of the street light.

"His," Mark said, and pointed his thumb over his shoulder at me.

Suddenly, a mop topped girl with pink hair exploded out of nowhere and repeatedly yelled 'happy birthday' while she threw handfuls of confetti-sized glitter onto me. The scattershot crew of bike riding hippie kids spontaneously stopped dancing and ignited into the rowdiest ever version of Happy Birthday. When they reached the third line the entire group leaned in as one and held the note: "deeeeaaaaar--

Blond Nineteen stared intently at me, eyebrows up and gestured hands out as they all held the note and waited--

"Hank."

I said it fast and unsteady like I wasn't sure if it was the right answer, like I wasn't sure what came next--

"Haa-aaannnk, happy birthday to you!" The last word of the song was shouted like a cheer. There was a full moment empty of everything, a stillness like time had stopped as the song whipped out into the night air up toward the moon.

Before I could exhale a thank you, those crazy, dancing Neverland kids cheered and applauded as they formed an impromptu receiving line. Blond Nineteen stuck his hand out for a formal handshake. When I took his hand he pulled me into a long, tight hug. Glitter Girl placed her hand on my heart and whispered, "long life" into my ear before she tossed one last handful of glitter into the air above me and shimmied away. One by one every person there came up to me and showered me with hugs and kisses and wishes and blessings.

Someone restarted the music at the rickshaw and as if practiced, a large circle formed. The speakers sprayed music over us and a beach style hora began. A boy who had introduced himself as Serge, with a dusty mop of hair that had long ago escaped any taming, bounced into the circle a shirtless teen-aged god fever dancing only happiness. Blond Nineteen and Glitter Girl joined in. Everyone danced, arms entwined while laughing and singing. People hopped into the center of the circle, twisted and turned and slide back out. Glitter sparked on our sweaty faces, glitter sparkled on the ground below our feet.

After several songs, the circle broke apart. People began to dance their way out onto the sand, bodies spinning, hopping, swaying, all led by Serge, a twirling dizzy force unto himself. Mark, Bryan, Joe and I said our goodbyes and began to walk back toward the pier. I was buzzing and tingling and felt very much alive.

Bryan slid his arm through Mark's arm and said, "I can't believe that just happened."

"I'm not exactly sure what did happen," Mark said.

I turned and looked back to prove to myself that something had happened, to make sure that there ever had been a group of blissed out dancing kids there in the first place. Under the lone street lamp was the rickshaw and the herd of waiting bicycles. To my left the moon hung over the bay and reflected light on the water. Faint silhouettes at the shore played at the water's edge, their whoops and laughter mixed with the sound of the nighttime surf and skipped across the sand up to where I stood on the bike path.

A quiet realization washed over me like I was body surfing in the dark water with those kids. What had happened was that I had just received a magical baptism from a traveling nighttime tribe who had so much youth they had to share it with me.

I turned back and looked at Joe. There were pieces of glitter in his hair, on his face. I reached out and picked a big green star stuck to his cheek. I looked at from the star to Joe to the beach and back.

"What an amazing birthday, I said as I shook my head in wonder.

Joe grinned, pulled me tight and said, "Hello, fifty."

OCTOBER

HALLOWEEN:
"TRICKS AND TREATS"
BY WARNER DAVIDSON

"**C**aleb Alan Stone! Get down off that chair before you break your neck!" Tyler McKenzie was exhausted after another long shift shelving books at the library and he was in no mood for the antics of a 4-year-old. Caleb, on the other hand, was wound up like a top … a top on amphetamines.

"I need another cookie."

"No, you don't *need* another cookie. You've had enough sugar today."

Tyler grabbed the squirming boy by the waist and set him down on the kitchen floor, maybe a little harder than he'd intended. He slid the chair away from the counter and moved it back underneath the table from the spot where Caleb had taken it.

"But I *want* a cookie, Uncle Ty." Caleb grabbed the chair again and started sliding it back across the room.

"No, I said! It'll spoil your appetite!" Tyler grabbed the back of chair and wrestled it away from the 4-year-old, returning it once again to its proper place. This time, he secured it with his foot so Caleb couldn't move it. "Just go into the other room and play while I finish making your dinner. It's your favorite—a grilled cheese sandwich with mustard and pickles, and cream of tomato soup."

"*I want a cookie!*" It was more a shriek than words. Caleb slugged Tyler's thigh with his bunched up little fist.

Tyler grabbed Caleb gently by the shoulders and crouched down so that he was eye-level with the boy. He took a deep breath to calm himself before speaking.

"Caleb," he said using his best authority figure tone, "you know that tomorrow is Halloween, right? And you also know that if you don't behave yourself, I'll have to tell your dad when he gets home. And you know what that means, don't you? If he finds out you've been misbehaving again, he won't let you go trick-or-treating."

Tears welled up in Caleb's eyes. "But … but you promised me, Uncle Ty."

"I promised I'd take you trick-or-treating if you were a good boy. Do you think this is how good boys behave?"

Caleb scuffed his feet and looked down at the floor. "No," he said quietly, wiping his eyes on the back of his hand.

Tyler kissed the boy on the forehead and tousled his hair. "Tell you what, Sport, if you do what I tell you for the rest the night, I won't say anything to your dad, okay?"

Caleb nodded his head slowly.

"Good. Go on and play now. Dinner will be ready in a few minutes. Afterward, you can show me your Halloween costume. And if you're extra special good, I'll read you a story after your bath."

"If I'm extra special good can I have extra pickles on my samich too?"

"Of course you can."

Tyler closed his eyes and exhaled his relief as the boy scampered off to the living room to play with his Lego set.

How did I get myself into this?

* * *

It was just after 10:30 p.m., and Tyler sat quietly on the sofa reading a book. He heard a key slip gently into the lock of the apartment door. The door opened and in walked his roommate—and Caleb's dad—Aaron Stone, his gym bag in one hand and a protein shake in the other.

"Hey, Aaron. You're home late tonight."

As always, Tyler was struck by how awesome Aaron looked, even dressed in sweaty gym clothes as he was now.

"Hey Ty. It was so busy today that I never got a chance to work out, so after I closed up the gym, I stayed on a bit longer and got a quick workout when there was no one there to distract me. Now I'm completely wiped." Aaron was the night manager of Ripped, the trendiest gym in town. As part of the agreement they made when Tyler rented a room in Aaron's condo, Aaron gave Tyler full membership privileges at Ripped free of charge and, in exchange, Tyler watched Caleb whenever Aaron had to work nights and weekends. It was a win for all three of them. Especially for him, Tyler thought, because he would never have been able to afford a membership at a swanky place like Ripped on his part-time wages from the library and the stipend he was paid as a graduate research assistant at George Washington University.

"Take a load off." Tyler patted the sofa next to himself and Aaron sat down beside him.

"I was just going to grab a beer. You want anything?"

"Yeah, if you don't mind. I'd love a cold one."

"Coming right up."

Tyler jumped up off the sofa and padded barefoot into the kitchen. He got two bottles of Sam Adams from the refrigerator, opened them both, and then returned to the living room. He handed one bottle to Aaron and sat down beside him once again on the sofa.

"Thanks, Ty." Aaron took a long pull from the bottle and sighed heavily. "Did Caleb give you much grief tonight?"

"Not really. He got a little wound up earlier, and we had a bit of a tussle just before dinnertime because I wouldn't let him have another cookie—he'd already devoured three. By the way, the cookie jar is nearly empty again. That kid of yours has got some sweet tooth. Anyway, he started pitching a fit and we had a heart-to-heart about whether or not I'd be taking him trick-or-treating tomorrow if he didn't behave. He calmed right down. I don't think he remembers last year at all so this whole Halloween thing is still all new to him. He's really excited."

Tyler paused for a moment before he continued. "By the way, Caleb is totally adorable in that Spider-Man costume you got for him. I had a hard time convincing him not to wear it to bed tonight."

"I guess I'm going to have to hide that cookie jar … and thanks, by the way, for being so good to him. He adores you and he really loves spending time with you. I've been worried about him ever since Perry's … accident. He was so withdrawn at first that I was getting concerned he'd never open up to anyone ever again. But then you came along, and you're so good with him, and I think he's going to be fine." Aaron, and his lover Perry Green, had adopted Caleb when he was only a few months old. Tragically, Perry was killed in a car accident just over a year ago. A drunk driver swerved into his lane on the George Washington Parkway and both cars collided head-on. Perry, they said, died instantly. Tyler had never met him but he could tell that Aaron still grieved for Perry, though he rarely talked about him. He admired the way Aaron stayed strong for Caleb but he hoped one day Aaron would be able to get past his own grief as well. He deserved that much after everything he'd been through. Tyler wasn't certain that if he ever lost someone as close to him as Aaron had, he could keep it all together like Aaron did. He was glad to do whatever he could to make Aaron's and Caleb's lives a little easier.

"Caleb seems to be doing much better these days," Tyler said. "He's much more social now than he was when I first moved in. Have you seen how well he plays with the other kids at the park now?"

Aaron nodded. A look of deep sorrow hung on his face as he picked at the label on the beer bottle and his eyes glassed over with unshed tears.

To dispel the sudden pall that had settled over them, Tyler patted Aaron's thigh a couple of times and asked, "So … how was your day?"

It worked. Aaron perked up a little and even managed a slight smile.

"Other than busy? It was fine I guess. Business as usual. The gym was pretty packed for a Thursday. Our membership is way up—so much so the owners are now considering opening up a second gym in the neighborhood. They're looking at a building over on 15th Street so it would be a lot closer to home. I really hope they get it."

He took another drink of his beer. "By the way, I saw your boyfriend again tonight."

"My boyfriend? I don't have a boyfriend. What do you mean?"

"Clay Matthews."

Tyler's heart skipped at beat at the mention of Clay's name. Clay Matthews was, perhaps, the hottest guy Tyler and ever seen.

"*Clay Matthews*? Why do you say he's my boyfriend? I hardly know the guy."

"C'mon Ty. Everyone knows you got it bad for him. And guess what … he asked about you tonight."

"He asked about me?"

"He sure did."

"What did he want to know?"

"He asked me if we—you and I—were a couple."

"So, basically, he was hitting on *you*."

"Nope. When he found out we weren't together like that, he asked if *you* were seeing anyone else. And he seemed quite happy when I told him you're still on the market."

"Oh, c'mon Aaron. You're puttin' me on. What would a guy like him want with me? He's gorgeous, he's got a great body, and a killer smile. Rumor has it that he owns some kind of software company ... they say he's got a buttload of money ... and ... did I mention he's got a really hot body?"

"I seem to recall you saying something about it, yeah." Aaron grinned. "By the way, I've also seen him in the locker room. He's got a dick the size of Long Island."

"I've noticed. The man is perfect in just about every way imaginable... and I'm just some science nerd who can barely make rent each month. No way he'd be interested in me. Besides, I've never spoken more than a few words at a time to him. In fact, I can barely speak to him at all."

"What do you mean you can barely speak to him at all?"

"Literally, I can't speak when I'm around him. I get all tongue-tied. He intimidates the hell out of me."

"Why should he intimidate you? You're a good looking guy. You've got a pretty nice physique yourself, even if you do cover it up with clothes that are way too big for you."

"I don't know. He just does. And I like loose-fitting clothes, they're more comfortable. Besides, it seems to me that he's more your league than mine."

"Don't be silly, Ty. And don't put yourself down like that. You're just as good looking as he is. And I'm telling you that it's *you* he's interested in, not me."

"Wanna bet on it?"

"You'd lose, and I'm not taking your money just for sport. First off, everyone at Ripped, including Clay Matthews, knows that I'm far from ready to start dating again ... if I ever do. It's just way too soon after ..." He didn't complete the thought.

"That doesn't mean he's not going to try."

"Think for just a moment about what you're saying. If he was hitting on me, why would he ask me about you, rather than asking me about me? He's into you, Ty, I know it. Why is that so hard for you to believe?"

"I just think you're wrong about him, that's all."

"Well, promise me one thing."

"What's that?"

"When he asks you out, just say yes."

"He's not going to ask me out."

"*Just promise!*"

"Okay, I promise ... but he's not going to ask."

* * *

Tyler arrived home after his shift at the library not long before Aaron was due to leave for work. According to his trusty Timex, it was 3:35 p.m., plenty of time to wind down before trick-or-treating time, which was set to begin at 4:00. Tyler, of course, was old enough to remember the good, old days when trick-or-treating didn't begin until after the sun went down. In today's world that was simply too dangerous—a shame, really, since it took a lot of the spooky fun out of the holiday.

As soon as he let himself into the apartment, Caleb met him at the door. The boy was barefoot but already dressed in his Spider-Man costume. An orange plastic candy pail, with a jack-o-lantern face painted on it, dangled from his little hand.

"Can we go tricks-or-treating now, Uncle Ty?"

"Caleb, you know that trick-or-treating doesn't start until 4 o'clock. We talked about this last night."

Aaron, who appeared just then in the kitchen doorway, admonished his son, "Caleb, give your Uncle Ty a few moments to sit down and relax. He just walked in the door, for goodness sake, and he's probably tired."

"But Daddy, if we wait too long, they might run out of candy."

"Trust me. There'll be plenty of candy when you get out there. Just cool your jets for awhile and give Uncle Ty some breathing room."

He paused before continuing.

"Thanks, Ty, for taking him out tonight. And Caleb? Be a good boy for Uncle Ty … do whatever he tells you, okay? Remember to hold onto Ty's hand … and no running into the street."

"Okay Daddy."

"Now come over here and give your Daddy a kiss. I've got to leave for work." Aaron picked Caleb up and kissed him on the forehead. "Okay Sport … have fun tonight. Daddy will see you in the morning."

Aaron left the apartment, closing the door behind him.

Tyler set his book bag on the floor just inside the door to his bedroom and then sat down on the sofa. Immediately Caleb jumped up and huddled up close to him.

They sat there quietly for about 30 seconds.

"Do you have enough breathing room yet, Uncle Ty?"

Tyler laughed. "Yes, Caleb, I have enough breathing room."

"Then can we go tricks-or-treating now?"

Tyler laughed again, shaking his head, looking at his watch again. This time it read 3:45.

"Go on … go put your shoes on."

In a flash, Caleb jumped off the sofa and sprinted into his room.

* * *

It was on the warm side for late October and Tyler thought that was a very good thing indeed. He could only imagine the scene that would have ensued if he'd had to insist that Caleb put a jacket on over his Spider-Man costume.

As they walked hand-in-hand down the sidewalk … scratch that … as Caleb *pulled* him down the sidewalk by the hand, Tyler was amazed by the sheer number of miniature witches, goblins, wizards, and superheroes out filling their coffers with sweets, escorted by adoring mothers and fathers. It was not at all surprising to Tyler that same-sex couples accompanied many of these energetic, young trick-or-treaters. This was the gayborhood after all. Most of these parents probably thought that he was Caleb's father. He found that thought surprisingly pleasing.

Tyler and Caleb made their way through the neighborhood, stopping only at the houses where a porch light or yard light were burning—the tacit indicator that Halloween treats were available inside. As they approached each new door, Tyler would stand off to the side while Caleb rang the bell and shouted out, "tricks or treat," just like Tyler had taught him—well almost just like. And each time the occupant of the house deposited candy into Caleb's plastic jack-o-lantern, Caleb would say, "Thank you," like a perfect little gentlemen. Tyler couldn't have been prouder if he were Caleb's real father. As they retreated from each house, Caleb would look up at him, wide-eyed and grinning from ear-to-ear, and say to Tyler, "Did you see what I got, Uncle Ty? Did you see what I got?"

It was times like this when Tyler thought that maybe … one day … when he had someone special in his life … maybe it wouldn't be such a bad thing to have a kid of his own.

By 4:45 Caleb's jack-o-lantern pail was getting a bit full—and a bit too heavy—for a small boy to carry, so as they walked from house to house, Tyler carried it for him. They had been trick-or-treating for nearly an hour and now there was only one more house on the block that they had not yet visited.

"Caleb," Tyler prepared himself for another outburst, "when we're done with this block, I think we should call it a day. You've already got quite a lot of candy there."

"Just one more, okay Uncle Ty?"

Much relieved Tyler nodded his agreement.

When they got to that last house, Tyler was pleased to see the gaslight out front was burning. He opened the wrought iron gate and held it open so Caleb could walk through it. Tyler handed the boy his candy pail and he turned back to secure the gate behind him. When he looked forward again, he beheld for the first time a large, two-story house made of red brick, its large windows trimmed in white. He couldn't name the architectural style but Tyler guessed the house must have been at least 200 years old, if not older, and it was magnificent.

Four steps up from ground level was a large front porch with a roof over it and, on the porch, were at least ten children, dressed in various guises, standing in wait to receive their candy treat. The man, who apparently lived in this magnificent house, cradled a large orange bowl in his hands. Tyler looked up at him and froze in his tracks.

It was Clay Matthews.

His first instinct was to turn around and run in the other direction, making a quick getaway before Clay spotted him. Just as he was about to turn and go, Caleb grabbed him by the hand again and tugged him eagerly forward along the flagstone walk in the direction of the porch. They were passed along the way by the Little Mermaid and a diminutive Darth Vader who were headed in the opposite direction. The children giggled excitedly as they pushed open the gate and skipped off down the street, letting it slam shut behind them.

And that's when it happened … Tyler turned back toward the house. And Clay Matthews was looking right at him … and he was grinning from ear-to-ear.

So much for that quick get-away!

* * *

Before Tyler could stop him, Caleb dropped his hand and bounded up the steps of Clay Matthews' house to wait his turn at the back of the line of costumed children. Tyler, having no other choice, followed, his anxiety increasing with every step.

Meanwhile, at the top of the stairs Clay handed each child in line a candy bar that, Tyler noted, was just about the size of a small aircraft carrier. Clay made a point of telling each child how wonderful his or her costume was. Through it all Clay never broke eye contact with him and Tyler's face grew hotter with each passing second. He could hear his heart beating in his ears and, suddenly, his tongue felt like old shoe leather and two sizes too big for his mouth. He knew that if he had to converse with Clay right now he'd make a complete fool of himself.

Then, finally, it was Caleb's turn for a treat.

"Tricks or treat," Caleb said, beaming up at Clay.

Clay crouched down so that he was now eye-level with Caleb.

"Well, hello there Spider-Man! It's such a pleasure to meet you." He shook Caleb's hand.

"I'm not the real Spider-Man," Caleb whispered conspiratorially.

Clay feigned surprise. "But you're so big and strong. C'mon … you *must* be the real Spider-Man."

Caleb giggled. "This is just a Halloween costume. My name is Caleb Alan Stone and I'm almost 5."

Well, it's a pleasure to meet you, Caleb Alan Stone. I'm Clayton Samuel Matthews … but you can call me Clay."

He paused.

"Listen … Spider-Man … I mean Caleb … as you can see, my bowl is empty and I have to go inside to get some more candy. Would you and your father like to come inside with me, maybe have a glass of lemonade? It's really good … I made it myself." He looked up at Tyler and smiled broadly this time, revealing a perfect set of white teeth.

Tyler's insides melted.

"That's not my daddy. That's Uncle Ty."

"Well … would you and Uncle Ty care to join me?"

Caleb looked up at Tyler.

Clay looked up at Tyler.

Tyler looked back and forth between Caleb and Clay.

"Sure," he said finally, "we'd like that." Tyler wasn't sure how he'd mustered the courage to speak.

Clay stood up then, grabbed Caleb's hand, and escorted him inside. Tyler followed them across the threshold and closed the door behind him.

Once inside, Clay escorted them into a very well-appointed living room, that Tyler noted, was furnished in an ultra-modern style that somehow did not look at all out of place in such an old house. He also noticed a number of pieces of art that he was sure were not reproductions. The rumors about Clay Matthew's affluence, it appeared, were true.

Clay extended his hand to Tyler. "I see you at the gym all the time, but we've never been formally introduced. I'm Clay Matthews."

Tyler shook his hand. His grip was strong and confident.

"Tyler ... Tyler McKenzie."

"It's a pleasure to finally meet you Tyler McKenzie."

"Nice to meet you too."

Clay gestured toward the sofa. "Make yourself at home, gentlemen. Excuse me for a moment while I'll go retrieve that chocolate bar for Spider-Man and pour us each a glass of cold lemonade."

Tyler sat on the sofa and Caleb snuggled up close to him.

A moment later Clay returned with a tray on which were three glasses of lemonade. He set the tray down on the coffee table in front of the sofa and handed a glass to Caleb.

"Here you go Spider-Man ... I mean Caleb. Are you *sure* you're not Spider-Man?"

Caleb giggled and took the glass.

"What do you say?" Tyler asked him.

"Thank you."

"You are very welcome Caleb."

Clay handed a glass to Tyler and picked up his own.

"Thank you."

"You are very welcome as well, Tyler McKenzie." That smile again. Tyler flushed and looked down at the floor.

Caleb took a sip of his lemonade, scrunched his face up at the tartness and shuddered.

"If it's too sour for you, Caleb, I can add more sugar."

"No … I like it just like this," Caleb smiled broadly. "It tastes just like sour balls Daddy buys for me at the movies."

They were silent for a moment and Clay sat down next to Tyler on the sofa, angling his body sideways so that they almost faced each other.

"So Caleb is your nephew?"

"Actually, no. He's Aaron Stone's son. You know Aaron … one of the managers of Ripped? He's my roommate."

"Right. I know Aaron. I also knew that you two lived together, but I didn't know Aaron was a father. Funny, we've talked many times—in fact, we talked just last night—and he never mentioned having a son."

Tyler glanced quickly at Caleb, who was engrossed in his lemonade. "Aaron really doesn't talk much at all about his personal life. It's a long story."

Tyler paused, glancing down at Caleb and then back up at Clay again, signaling with his eyes that this probably wasn't the best time to go into it with Caleb in the room.

Taking Tyler's cue, Clay let the subject drop and Tyler continued. "I look after Caleb when Aaron has to work nights or weekends. Aaron has enrolled him in daycare Monday through Friday so Caleb's got someone with him all the time."

"That's awfully nice of you to do—especially since you and Aaron aren't *involved* … as a couple or anything."

"It's nothing, really. Aaron gives me a break on the rent, plus my membership at Ripped. I couldn't afford it otherwise. Besides, Aaron and Caleb are like family to me now."

"So, Tyler … tell me about yourself. What do you do when you're not at the gym?"

"I'm a graduate student at GWU ... and I work part time at the undergraduate library."

"What do you study?"

"I'm working on my PhD ... molecular biology."

"Wow! I'm impressed. Forgive my ignorance—I know very little about science—what will you do when you're finished?"

"I'd like to do research ... maybe teach. Nothing very exciting, I'm afraid."

"That sounds pretty exciting to me ... and, I'd guess, pretty important work."

Tyler, who was getting uncomfortable talking about himself, especially to Clay Matthews, redirected the conversation. "What ... what do you do? I mean ... when you're not at the gym?"

"Not a whole lot these days. I had my own business for a number of years but I sold it, just this past week in fact. I thought I'd take a couple of months off before deciding what to do with the rest of my life."

"You can do that? Take a couple of months off?" Tyler regretted asking as soon as the words came out of his mouth. "I'm sorry. That was really rude of me. You don't have to answer that."

"No, it's all right. It's no secret. I was a software engineer. Long story short, I developed a couple of computer applications that turned out to be perfectly suited for small businesses. I sold a couple of them and made a bit of money. I used it to form a software start-up company that developed and marketed new software products for a variety of purposes. It was a slow start, but eventually business began to pick up, and after the first year or so, we started turning a profit—much more than I ever dreamed possible. Unfortunately, the flip side of that kind of quick success is that it takes over your life ... *completely*. The more products I sold, the more new ones they wanted. Before long, the business was gobbling so much of my time that I no longer had any left for a personal life—no time for family or friends, no boyfriend, not even an occasional date. When I wasn't sleeping or at the gym, I was working. Toward the end it was even getting hard to make time to work out on a regular basis, and regular workouts were the only thing keeping me sane. The stress was overwhelming and, truth told, it was a rather lonely way to live. And what good is all that success and money when I've got no one to share it with?"

"That does sound pretty dreadful. Funny, though, I would never have associated the word 'lonely' with you. Every time I've ever seen you, you've always had a big smile on your face. I guess that's another lesson for me about making assumptions."

"Those smiles were for you, Tyler!"

Tyler didn't think it was possible, but his face got even hotter and, he was sure, a deep shade of crimson. If he noticed, Clay was courteous enough not to mention it.

"When Beta Tech approached me last month about buying me out," he continued, "I jumped at the chance."

"What about now? Are you still happy with that decision?"

"No regrets at all … and I plan to take full advantage of the fact that I'm in control of my life again. Starting right now." He paused for a moment before continuing, "What time does Aaron get off work?"

"He's usually home by 9:30. Why?"

"I was just thinking that it would be really nice if you came back tonight after Aaron gets home."

"Back here? I'm not sure I follow you."

Clay flashed him that smile again. "For a date."

"A date?"

"Yeah, a date. You know, when two people who are attracted to each other spend time together … try to get to know one another better. Besides, it's Halloween, right? It's my favorite holiday and I, for one, don't want to spend it by myself. I was really happy when you two fine-looking men showed up on my doorstep in search of a Halloween treat. I've never seen you outside of the gym before so this is quite a pleasant surprise."

Clay paused a moment, as a mischievous grin spread across his face. "I really do love Halloween and all the little trick-or-treaters. It brings out the kid in me. But we're not so old yet that we can't have a little Halloween fun ourselves. Caleb, here, already has the chocolate bar I gave him earlier and a whole pail full of treats. I was kind of hoping that I could give *you* an extra special treat of your very own later on. If you don't have other plans, I mean." His smile transformed then from mischievous to flirtatious in the blink of an eye.

Tyler's face was on fire now.

"Can I have an extra special treat too?" Caleb asked suddenly, reminding Tyler that the 4-year-old was sitting next to him.

Clay laughed and said to Caleb, "How about another chocolate bar?"

Caleb nodded his head and clapped his hands together, grinning from ear to ear.

Clay got up and went into the kitchen.

Tyler sat there, quietly on the outside but reeling on the inside from what had just happened. He realized that he'd just had an entire conversation with Clay Matthews and his heart hadn't stopped beating at all ... and he hadn't made a fool of himself even once. In fact, Clay Matthews had just asked him out on a date ... and he could hardly believe it was real.

He remembered then his promise to Aaron.

Just then Clay came back from the kitchen with another chocolate bar for Caleb. He handed it to the boy who accepted it eagerly, and sat back down next to Tyler on the sofa.

"So, what do you say? Now that I've got my life back, I want to enjoy every minute of it ... starting tonight ... with you."

Tyler didn't respond right away.

"Tyler?"

"I can be here by 10:00."

After all, he couldn't renege on his promise to Aaron.

* * *

By 8:30, Caleb was already tucked safely in his bed, still wearing his Spider-Man costume. After an hour of trying to talk him into changing into his pajamas, Tyler finally gave up and gave in to him. As was their nightly ritual, as soon as Caleb was snuggled under the covers, Tyler sat in the chair next to his bed and read a story to him. Tonight's selection was *Harry the Dirty Dog*. It was one of Caleb's favorites and he'd practically memorized every word, but in less than ten minutes the 4-year-old was fast asleep. Clearly, the excitement of Halloween had worn him right out.

As soon as it was clear to Tyler that Caleb down for the night, he started getting ready for his date with Clay. Not knowing precisely what to expect, he decided to be prepared for any contingency. He showered and shaved, brushed and flossed his teeth, and made sure his hair was combed just right. He even put on a dab of Aaron's Acqua di Giò, taking extra care not to overdo it. It was expensive cologne, he was certain, but he knew that Aaron wouldn't mind just this once. After all, Tyler rationalized, he was only going through with this because he'd promised Aaron.

Yeah, right!

Even he couldn't convince himself that was true.

Deciding what to wear was another story. Aaron always kidded him about the way he dressed, telling him that the days of baggy pants were over, but after pulling almost every item of clothing he owned out of his closet, Tyler still couldn't make up his mind what to wear. He was still in his briefs pondering his options when he heard the front door open and shut. He looked at the clock next to his bed. It wasn't even 9:00 yet, a bit early for Aaron to be home. Next he heard the door to Caleb's room open, and then close once again, very gently.

A few moments later, Aaron appeared at *his* bedroom door and knocked on the doorframe.

"Knock, knock."

"Hey Aaron, you're home early. What's up?"

"The gym was dead tonight. But, I suppose, Halloween is always slow. People are busy with parties and such. I know of at least four big parties happening right now here in the neighborhood and all the bars, I imagine, are having their usual Halloween drink specials and costume contests. And then there's the high heel race on 17th Street. I got bored sitting there all alone in that big, empty gym, so I put a sign on the door, closed up early, and came home."

He paused. "What are you doing? It looks like you're getting dressed up to go somewhere. Don't tell me you're going to the high heel race! I, mean, it used to be fun until it became such a spectator event for curious heterosexuals."

"I *am* going out, but not to the high heel race. I have a date."

"A *date*? *You* have a date? Okay, tell me right now what have you done with the real Tyler McKenzie? The real Tyler McKenzie is way too busy to date anyone."

Tyler balled up a t-shirt and tossed it at Aaron and it bounced off his chest. Aaron picked it up off the floor and tossed it back.

"Who's the lucky guy? Don't tell me, let me guess … Clay Matthews."

"Ding, ding, ding … give that man a prize."

"What did I tell you?"

"Don't gloat … it's not a flattering color on you."

"So, where are you going on this date?"

"I don't know. I'm meeting him at his place at 10:00."

"Ahhhhh! *His* place! So it's a booty call."

"Your guess is as good as mine, but I really doubt it."

"It's a booty call … trust me. Wear something sexy."

"You're enjoying this, aren't you?"

"Immensely! What *are* you going to wear? I hope it's something that actually fits for a change."

"I don't know. Help me pick something."

Aaron grabbed a pair of gray twill jeans off the bed and tossed them at Tyler. "Wear these. They show off your sexy butt. Matthews won't be able to keep his hands off you."

Tyler stepped into the jeans, pulled them up, buttoned the waist and zipped up the fly. He turned around and looked in the mirror.

"I don't know ... they 're kind of snug."

"Trust me. You look great in them. Now for a shirt ... let me think ..."

Aaron paused tapping his index finger on his chin.

"I got it. Be right back."

Aaron turned and left the room. Tyler could hear him rustling about in his own room across the hall. He returned in less than a minute with a blue print shirt on a hanger. Tyler recognized it as the English Laundry shirt Aaron had ordered online just a couple of weeks earlier.

"Here ... put this on. I think it'll go great with those pants."

"Aaron, that's your new shirt. You haven't even worn it yourself yet. Look, the tag is still on it."

"Just take it Ty!" He ripped the tag off and handed the shirt to Tyler. Tyler slipped it on and buttoned it up the front.

Aaron stood back and appraised the results. "See, I told you it would be perfect. You look really hot, Ty."

"You think so?"

"Darlin', if I was looking for love, and I just met you in a bar dressed like that, I'd be all over you."

Tyler laughed.

"Clay Matthews is going to eat you up with a spoon."

* * *

A bit anxious and not knowing what to expect from the evening, Tyler arrived at Clay Matthews' house a few minutes early. Not wanting to appear overly eager, he walked around the block and arrived back at Clay's front gate a couple of minutes past 10:00. He entered the gate, walked up the flagstone path, climbed the porch stairs and walked across it to the front door. There was note, written in a neat, masculine script, taped to the door. Tyler read it:

Dear Tyler,
The door is unlocked. Please let yourself in. You'll find me, and
your Halloween surprise, at the end of the trail. I hope you like it.
Yours,
Clay

"The end of the trail?" Tyler said aloud to himself. "What on Earth could *that* mean?"

He took the note off the door, let himself in, and closed the door behind him. For safekeeping, he locked the deadbolt. As he turned back toward the interior of the house, he noticed a line of small votive candles, lit, illuminating the hallway in front of him.

Ah! So that's what he meant!

Tyler followed the trail of candles down the hall. About halfway down, the row of candles took a 180-degree turn and ascended the stairs to the second story of the house. Tyler followed it up the stairs. When he got to the top, the candle trail turned sharply again toward the front of the house. All the way at the end of the hall the row of candles stopped short in front of a door. Another note was affixed to the door at eye level. It was written in the same handwriting as before:

Knock three times and say, "Trick or treat?"

Rap, rap, rap. Tyler knocked on the door. "Trick or treat?"

The door opened slowly inward and standing behind it was Clay Matthews, clad only in a pair of jack-o-lantern briefs and a black bow-tie.

Booty call!

It appeared Aaron had been right about that part too.

Clay took Tyler by the hand and pulled him into the bedroom, closing the door behind them. Aside from Clay's perfect, nearly naked body, the first thing Tyler noticed about the room was that there were candles burning everywhere—and Clay looked sexier than hell in the soft glow of the candlelight.

Clay wrapped his left arm around Tyler's waist and pulled him close. Then he reached his right hand up and clasped it behind Tyler's neck, drawing him forward into a long, passionate kiss. Tyler accepted the embrace without resistance and fell into Clay's arms. The instant Clay's tongue parted his lips and mingled with his own, Tyler's cock began to swell and twitch.

By the time the kiss was over his erection—pinned tightly against the twill fabric of his pants in the hopeless tangle of his cotton briefs—ached for release. He took a step backward in vain attempt to dislodge it from its textile prison.

Clay, misunderstanding his withdrawal, stepped back as well. "Am I being too aggressive? I hope I'm not offending you."

"No ... not at all. You just caught me by surprise, that's all."

Clay looked down at Tyler's crotch. "From the looks of things, I assume it was a good surprise."

Tyler felt his face flush again. "Very."

Clay drew him in close again and kissed him tenderly this time. "Good. I didn't think you'd mind. For awhile now I've had a sense that you were interested in me but you were too shy to make a move. And like I said, I've been so wrapped up in my work that I didn't think it would be fair for me to make a move on you when I was in no position to date anyone seriously. But things are different now. I've sold my business. And when I talked to Aaron about you the other night, he said that you ...," he trailed off without finishing the sentence.

"What ... just what did Aaron have to say about me?"

"You really want to know?"

"Yeah, I'd like to know."

"It was excellent advice, really. Advice I fully intend to heed."

"What did he say?"

Clay smiled. "Just that you are totally hot for me ... and since you weren't ever going to do anything about it, I should just throw you down and fuck your brains out."

"*Oh ... my ... God*! Did he really say that?"

"Pretty much ... not in those exact words, maybe, but that was the gist of it."

Tyler laughed and shook his head. "I am *so* going to kill him."

"Okay ... so now that we're both clear on what's going to happen tonight ... are you ready for that throw down?"

"What are you waiting for?"

Clay grabbed Tyler by the waist and lowered him gently onto the bed.

* * *

He must have dozed off for a moment because Tyler suddenly found himself roused from sleep by the warm hand stroking his side. And then he remembered where he was ... in Clay Matthews' bed. He was lying on his left side and Clay was spooning him from behind.

The sex had been wonderful; the best Tyler had ever had. Clay was a gentle lover, and so generous. Tyler could not remember ever feeling so comfortable and at ease with another guy. It was like their bodies were made to fit together, like two adjoining pieces of a jigsaw puzzle. He couldn't believe this was that same man who, only hours before, had intimidated him so much he couldn't speak.

Tyler reached back and clasped the hand that was stroking him, and pulled it up and around his chest.

"Sorry, Ty ... I didn't mean to wake you. I just couldn't resist touching you."

"I didn't mean to fall asleep. What time is it?"

Clay propped himself up on his elbow to see the clock on the nightstand. "Almost the witching hour."

"I should probably get going and let you sleep."

"You're not going anywhere, Bucko. I'm not through with you yet. Besides, tomorrow's Saturday and I was hoping you'd stay the night ... unless you've got someplace else you have to be?"

"No ... no ... I'm not working tomorrow and Aaron is taking Caleb to see his grandmother first thing in the morning, so I've got no reason to get up early."

"Then it's settled."

He kissed the back of Tyler's neck before continuing. "Maybe ... if you don't have other plans ... we could spend the day together."

"I'd like that."

They snuggled some more.

"Ty?"

"Yeah?"

"I'm really glad you're here."

"Me too."

Clay rolled Tyler onto his back and kissed him deeply. He pulled back. "It's still Halloween you know. It's not too late for another treat."

"What, no tricks?"

"Tricks come ... and tricks go! You? I'm keeping. We've got a lot of lost time to make up for."

"You know, Clay, my life is in a bit of disarray at the moment, what with school and my job and looking after Caleb. Are you sure you really want to deal with all that?"

"This thing here—between you and me—this is a really good thing and I'm pretty certain it's well worth the effort. School is only temporary and patience is my middle name. As for Caleb, I really like kids. It wouldn't be such a terrible thing to have him around now and then. Besides, it'll be good practice. Who knows ... maybe one day, you and I will decide to have one of our own."

"This is only our first date, Clay. Aren't you getting a little ahead of yourself?"

"Maybe, but my gut says 'no.' Ty, from the first moment I saw you at the gym, I knew in my gut that you were the one."

"The one what?"

"The one I am going to spend the rest of my life with."

"You think so, huh? I have to warn you, most of the guys I've dated haven't stuck around longer than a couple of weeks."

Clay laughed. "Twenty years from now, I'll remind you that you said that. And those other guys? They must have been nuts."

"So, this wasn't just a booty call?"

"No, it wasn't. I have to admit, you *do* have a nice booty ... but it's *you* I really want, Ty. Now shut up and kiss me, it's almost midnight and I've got one more Halloween treat for you."

Tyler kissed him ... and the treat he got in return was *so* much better than chocolate.

NOVEMBER

THANKSGIVING:
"HAPPY FAMILY MOMENT"
BY JON MACY

HAPPY FAMILY MOMENT

JON MACY

ALL I COULD THINK ABOUT WAS THAT THIS WOULD BE THE LAST TIME I EVER HAD THANKSGIVING WITH MY FAMILY.

THEN, FROM THE END OF THE TABLE, MY GRAND MOTHER CHIMED IN ON THE DEBATE.

LET ME TELL YOU ABOUT WHAT WE WOULD DO FOR OUR YOUNG MEN ABOUT TO GO OFF TO WAR.

BRAVE YOUNG MEN WHO MIGHT NOT RETURN.

BUT WE COULDN'T RISK GETTING PREGNANT.

DECEMBER

HANUKKAH:
"THE HANUKKAH GIFT"
BY DAVID BERGER

Author's Note: Story takes place prior to "Father's Day" story.

December 22, 2011

"Come on, Aaron. Let me introduce you to my friend Kelly," said Janice. "I've told her all about you." He could tell she'd already had a few glasses of Chianti.

Aaron Feldman didn't have a chance when he walked through the door of Giovanni's, the Italian restaurant where East Boston High School always held its holiday party.

Right in the heart of Boston's Italian North End, Giovanni's catered to a healthy mix of Beantown's upper crust and its working class, and teachers loved to frequent Friday happy hour, especially when they paid half price. This time of year, schools from all over the city vied for the best day just before the holidays were in full swing to have their get-togethers here. Some said the draw was the dark mahogany framing out the interior; others said it was the eclectic yet approachable menu. Tonight, however, the draw was the buffet and the open bar from eight to eleven.

At this moment, though, Aaron was wishing he'd just brought home take-out Kosher Chinese from Fung Wa's. Janice Wilkins had been trying for months to get him to meet her friend, Kelly, a bartender at Sammy's down on Commonwealth Ave. Aaron taught across the hall from Janice, a woman with as much tact as a steamroller, and they developed a variety of friendship not long after she arrived at the beginning of the school year that Aaron affectionately referred to as "arms length." While some might call Janice crude, most just knew that her "inner Brooklyn" was her outer persona, but she knew how to teach freshman English like no one else. Always just shy of inappropriate, she had this knack of saying the right thing to get her students on task or quiet, but her students loved her. Aaron, right now... not so much.

Even though he was in his seventh year of teaching at East Boston High, a pretty progressive school for its downtown location, Aaron had remained closeted so as not to make waves. He normally just closed his classroom door and taught his AP English classes, doing his best not to get caught up in teacher lounge gossip or after school cliques, things that Janice reveled in. At fifty-one, she had the spunk of a woman half her age and tried to dress that way, too. During class, she put her short, auburn hair up in a clip, but now, out in public, she desperately wanted her hair to look like Angelina Jolie or Joan Crawford; she could never decide which one she liked better. Tonight, she wore black leggings with a burgundy Christmas sweater she simply adored, although most people thought the holly leaf sequin appliqués were a bit over the top. Having basically accosted Aaron and brought him to the event room in the back of the restaurant to meet Kelly, Janice felt this sense of accomplishment having finally brought them together to talk.

Servers came around with pigs in a blanket or cheese cubes—the best the school could afford since they spent more money on the buffet and bar—and Aaron quietly wished he could be whisked away on a tray, somewhere other than where he was. Kelly seemed pleasant enough, her short, red hair swaying as she talked. She tended to talk with her hands, and on a few occasions, her whiskey sour almost spilled on Aaron, making an awkward situation that much more unnerving. He had been to his share of school gatherings and district functions, so he had mastered the ability of the "interested head bounce" with the occasional "knowing smile," not to be outdone by the "agreeable chuckle."

"So, Janice tells me you're an English teacher. I'd better watch my grammar, huh," she said, sipping her drink.

Not like I haven't heard that one before, thought Aaron. "Oh, I'm 'off duty', so no worries," he said, smiling.

Kelly's laugh was a combination of a guinea pig's squeal and hiccups. For a while Janice stood with them, but when she saw some other people she just had to talk to, she waved to them and then meandered her way through the crowd.

"I'm glad that Janice suggested we meet," Kelly said. "You seem real nice. And, Janice is a doll. Her and I go way back."

It took all the power he could muster not to cringe with that grammar mistake. *Her and I. Really?* He thought. Aaron hated to be a grammar snob, but some things he felt people should just know; he politely kept tight-lipped. Since she had had a few drinks, Kelly would touch him on the arm when she talked, something that predicted disaster for the evening because he knew the next usual step would be for her to move closer to him with the hope that he would eventually want to get her number or make her breakfast. After about ten more minutes of politeness, he needed a break.

"Hey," he began, gently cutting Kelly off, "I'd like to get another drink. Do you need anything?

She giggled and shook her head. As soon as he left the room, she sought out Janice to tell her how much she thought they hit it off.

Toward the front of the restaurant was the bar, and Aaron gestured to the bartender as he sat.

"Shot of Jameson, please. Better yet, make that a shot with a Guinness chaser."

He played with the shot glass a little, taking in his moment of rest, and downed the contents.

"Not enjoying the party?" asked the bartender, snatching the empty shot glass.

Aaron's expression answered the question.

"Yeah, holiday parties can be a bit much. They go on way too long, and either you eat too much or drink too much. Maybe it'll get better for you."

Once in a while, a guy would walk by the bar, give Aaron the once over, smile at him, and walk back into the back part of the restaurant, but Aaron wasn't having it. He didn't want to pick someone up at the holiday party. Even if he did, he'd have to make excuses to people if he wanted to leave with the guy, and that would just be awkward. Not being out did make his life harder, but he just thought it was for the best. Being single, too, in a city with hundreds of gay men didn't help, but as soon as he mentioned he was a teacher, it was the same routine: how fantastic he was for working with kids, how noble, but it would always come down to money. Teachers didn't make as much, so ultimately the guy would sweetly excuse himself from conversation to find someone else whose salary had more respectability. At least that was what the last guy he met told him.

A down-to-earth man in his early 30s, Aaron took good care of himself, although he wasn't the gym addict that some of his friends were. His mother had wanted to him to settle down with a "nice, Jewish girl" and have children, but coming out put an end to that for her. Ever since then, she felt it was her duty to find herself the best man she could for her son, but sometimes her overzealousness caused some misfires. Then, of course, Janice stepped into the picture, trying to work her "yenta magic" as his mother would say. Being a busybody was a pastime for Janice, and Aaron could usually deflect her, but this holiday party, she was determined to set him up with Kelly. So, now he sat at a bar, looking out over the mildly inebriated crowd, hoping he could just make it a little while longer. Once, when he saw Kelly looking for him, he pretended to be on a phone call.

He felt a slight chill and instinctively looked over to see someone had just entered the restaurant. The guy looked a little out of place, as if he were not sure he was supposed to be there, but he hung his grey wool overcoat on the rack and headed for the bar. Aaron kept peeking over at him, and when he was caught, the man gave that head lift men do when they acknowledge someone. Nick, the bartender, brought the man a Guinness without even asking what he wanted, so this guy had to be a regular. Aaron lifted his pint in a silent cheer; the man reciprocated before taking a healthy sip. When the guy reached to grab some pretzels, Aaron saw what he thought was a small yarmulke clipped to his head. He instantly smiled to himself.

"I'm Jason," the man said, holding out his hand. "Always good to meet another Guinness lover."

Aaron shook his hand firmly. "Aaron. Yeah, the best stout there is," he said. He looked away quickly.

After a few more handfuls of pretzels, Jason said, "You seem uncomfortable. Everything okay?"

"Yeah," Aaron said, "Just been a long day, and I'm not feeling much of the *holiday* spirit. This is my school's holiday party." He gestured with his head back to the crowd. "They're in the Christmas spirit, and I'm sitting here with some Irish ones."

Jason's laugh was nothing like Kelly's, making Aaron blush a little.

"Well, I was supposed to meet some friends here for dinner, but I don't see them. Maybe they're just running late."

Conversing with Jason was nothing like talking to Kelly. Aaron didn't feel the obligation to nod and smile; he was genuinely interested and at ease.

The only problem was, he couldn't read Jason very well. Was he just being friendly, or was there something else there? He'd never met any Jewish men as observant as Jason, keeping his head covered, who were gay, but that didn't mean there weren't any. He also didn't want to get his hopes up, either.

Jason talked about being the director of a residential home for emotionally disturbed teenagers, those who all but fell through the cracks in Boston's child welfare system. A small facility of only ten teens, the program had a quick turnaround of staff, something that had added more stress to his life in the past few weeks. He told Aaron that if his phone rang, he'd have to answer since he was on call. Something about Jason seemed familiar, but not like Aaron had met him before. It was just a sense of camaraderie: both working with kids, both being Jewish, both liking Guinness. He decided to test the water a little.

"I'd imagine with a job like yours, your social life must really suffer."

"A little," Jason said. "I think being in a position like mine I'd just want to spend time with people who understood my situation, since I could be called away at any time to deal with a crisis. Our facility is 'hands on', so our counselors might need to physically restrain clients. When that happens, I need to go in and set up a clinical assessment. I do try to get out much, like tonight's dinner with friends." He checked his watch. "But, either they don't seem to able to tell time or I've been stood up."

"Ah. Then you're taking off?" Aaron said, holding back his disappointment. He was about to shake hands and say, *Nice chatting with you, Jason.*

At that precise moment, Jason's phone vibrated on the bar.

"Hang on a second," he said. "I have to take this."

Now that Jason was occupied, Aaron had a chance to look him over. He had to be about six feet tall, with an athletic build—his toned upper body definitely filled out his forest green mock turtleneck well. His short brown hair was framed by longer sideburns that reached the bottom of his ear. Even with the dim lighting, Aaron could see he had rich, brown eyes with flecks of gold and hazel. Jason stood up for a moment when the call seemed to get more animated; as he paced a little, Aaron caught sight of how good Jason looked in his khakis. Really good. After his call ended, Jason sat back down.

"Everything all right?" Aaron said.

"Yeah. One of our clients decided he didn't like his bedtime, so the counselor told him to call me. I'm his advocate in the house. He just came back from a home visit, so he's acting out a little now."

"I totally understand. They show us the worst sides of themselves because they trust us to take care of them."

Thirty minutes flew by before either one of them realized it was 10 p.m., but the party was still going. Aaron figured that Kelly had probably given up on him and had found someone else to spill drinks on. For a brief moment, he felt a twinge of regret, but then he looked over at Jason, totally enrapt in talking about how he came to be more of an observant Jew after living as an atheist for many years. Aaron's regret faded. Apparently, Jason's father, a Reform rabbi, had died when Jason was ten, so Jason's faith dwindled over the years since the one man who guided him toward spiritual growth was gone. He had lost faith in G-d for many years, until he just woke up one day and realized he was being selfish. During the fall of his senior year in college, he befriended some more observant Jews on campus, but he didn't want to become Orthodox. Their friendship had put him in touch with aspects of his life he had abandoned after his father's death. When it came time for Yom Kippur, the Jewish Day of Atonement, all of the emotions he had pent up since he was a child flooded out, and his friends were there to console him, letting him work through his grief. The day after, he started keeping his head covered and slowly, over the following weeks, worked up to keeping kosher. Fortunately, living in Boston now, he could find kosher food quite readily. Something Aaron realized was that Jason never talked about having been in any relationships. He just had to know. And then, Fate intervened.

Jason stopped talking for a moment. He kept looking down at the bar, playing with a broken pretzel.

"I haven't talked about that to anyone in a long time, over ten years, in fact."

"Let's talk about something else, then," Aaron said.

For a minute or two, Jason seemed to be lost in thought, and Aaron wanted to console him, but he just gave Jason his moment.

"No, I'm fine. Really," he said, softly. "I was just remembering my partner, Chaim. He was a fireman during 9/11. When he and I met, a few months prior, I had poured my heart out to him with the same story I just told you. It felt good to talk about it again. Thank you."

Aaron sensed there was more coming so he didn't respond, and Jason knew he needed to add one more detail to help Aaron understand.

"Chaim was inside the South Tower when it collapsed. He went in to save some people who were trapped in the stairwell."

For what seemed like hours, silence hovered over them, even with all the Christmas music from the house band, the chatter of voices, and the clanking of glasses. Aaron really wanted to do something to make Jason feel better. Every cell in his body screamed to him. But, he didn't want to overstep a boundary. But, at least he now knew what he had wanted to know since Jason first entered Giovanni's.

"So, what about you?" Jason said, in a happier voice than Aaron expected. "Anyone special in your life?"

Now it was Aaron's turn. Feeling that a door had been left open, he didn't feel apprehensive talking about his childhood, having lived with domineering parents who wanted him to marry a woman so his mother could have grandchildren. Being the eldest of three, and the only son, he had always felt obligated to fulfill his mother's dream that he carry on the family name. Dating women came easily to him, although he never could have sex with them—nothing more than heavy petting or kissing. Aaron apparently had a charisma that made the girls he knew want to date him: a warm smile, a comfortable sense of humor, and a desire to listen, but these relationships lasted only a few months at most. Something else dominated his thoughts when it came to intimacy, but he couldn't bring himself to say it aloud or even admit to himself. He'd had a friend in high school, someone who he fooled around with awkwardly—nothing more than mutually pleasuring each other. Even in college, when had befriended gays and lesbians, he couldn't even look these people in the face and be honest. It wasn't until after graduate school that he finally found the courage to come out.

The gold and hazel flecks in Jason's eyes mesmerized him, made him feel at ease. He wondered if maybe the Jameson shots and pints of Guinness had contributed to this, but this went beyond intoxication, at least from alcohol.

"So, was your mother disappointed that you're not married to a nice, Jewish girl with kids, a Volvo, and a picket fence?" Jason said, grinning.

"At first. She's fine with it now. When you said you had started keeping kosher, I wanted to tell you that I do, too. That made her a little happier since I was strengthening my Judaism. I think she thought I was going to become a rabbi." He laughed a little. "I've only had a few relationships over the years, and they all ended badly. My only regret is that I'm getting older, and I want to have children someday. How about you?"

"Actually, I have a three year old son named Aryeh. With my job demanding so much of my time, I didn't think a social life would allow me to meet someone who also wanted a child, so I adopted. Here's a picture of him."

Aaron noticed that Aryeh was wearing a little yarmulke.

"I told him I would stop by my mother's house after dinner tonight so I could bring him his Hanukkah gift. Tonight's the first night."

"Why didn't you just leave when you realized your friends weren't coming?" Aaron said. "If I had known that..."

"My parents are taking care of him tonight. I'm sure he's full of latkes and has worn out my mother playing dreidel. And, I wanted to stay, Aaron. I've enjoyed this."

Feeling his face flush, Aaron looked down at the bar. Then, he heard the voice he hadn't heard all night shouting from across the restaurant, although with the other sounds, it didn't seem as jarring.

"There you are!" Janice said. "I thought you'd gone home or met some other hot mama. I told Kelly that you were probably shmoozing with people. I think she really likes you."

Aaron didn't know what to say, so he just introduced them.

"Jason, this is Janice. She teaches across the hall from me, and she's been trying to set me up with her friend, Kelly."

Jason understood what Aaron's lack of words told him.

"Nice to meet you, Jason. You here with someone?"

"Janice, you're drunk," Aaron said, smiling, trying to hold her up.

"No shit, Sherlock," she said. "Have I mentioned I love mojitos?"

Jason tried not to laugh.

While Aaron dealt with her, Jason had a few moments and saw how Aaron's short, curly, blond hair caught the light. Now that Aaron was standing, Jason could see how cute he really was, in a preppy sort of way. His blue Oxford, its top button undone to show a small silver Star of David, fit snugly against an athletic frame and was tucked into his 501s. The finishing touch was brown penny loafers—*he even dresses like an English teacher*, Jason thought. They were around the same height, too, although Jason thought he might be a little taller.

All Aaron wanted to do was have Janice return to Kelly or someone else so he could talk more with Jason, but Janice was determined to match him up with someone; whether or not it was Kelly, it didn't matter. Sometimes being closeted really made his life miserable. He finally convinced her to go back to the party, and he would catch up with her later. When he returned to the bar, he was relieved that Jason was still there. He'd hoped that her antics hadn't scared her off.

"I am so sorry about that. She's relentless."

"I take it you're not out at work," Jason said.

Aaron shook his head. "I'm sure people would be fine, but I guess I've just never wanted to take the leap."

"I understand completely. When I became director, at the first staff meeting, I came out to the whole group. I told them, if they had a problem with that, they could leave."

"And?"

"No one left. We've had a few gay and lesbian kids in the house over the months, and it's actually been nice being able to mentor them a little."

Without missing a beat, they were talking again, like old friends. It was getting later, approaching 11:00, so Jason said he'd have to get going soon. But, he didn't really want the night to end.

"You know, Aaron, when I came in here tonight, I never thought I would meet someone like you. I didn't think I'd meet someone at all, actually, since I had dinner plans. I'm glad they didn't show. So, here's my thought—come to my mother's house for the last bit of the first night of Hanukkah. Have a few latkes, play some dreidel, and let's forget about Janice and Kelly."

"You're sure it's not too late?"

"Not at all. My parents are night owls. Besides, my sisters are probably there, too, and it'll be nice to talk to you without "Jingle Bells" playing."

Aaron didn't hesitate to say yes.

"And, thank you. You've given me one of the best Hanukkah gifts I could ask for tonight," Jason said.

"What'd I do?"

"Throughout this whole evening of conversation, you've made me realize that just because I'm a workaholic father doesn't mean I can't meet someone."

Aaron didn't know how to respond. He grabbed his coat and Jason's off the rack. Just as they were about to walk out, they heard a familiar voice, a loud one.

"Hey! Where you going? Kelly said she'd like to chat with you some more. She really likes you." If Janice was anything, she was tenacious.

They turned around to see both Kelly, drink in hand, and Janice. Kelly's smile brought back that uncomfortable feeling for Aaron. What could he do? Jason saw the pained expression on Aaron's face and couldn't bear it any longer. Before Aaron knew what was happening, Jason put his arm around Aaron's neck, pulled him close, and kissed him—passionately. Without thinking, Aaron wrapped his arms around him, allowing himself to be kissed, not caring what might happen. It didn't last more than a few seconds, but it was enough to send the message. Janice and Kelly, both a little stunned, just stood there. Well, Janice wobbled a little.

Aaron said, "What was that for?"

"That was your Hanukkah gift," Jason said.

Leaning his forehead against Jason's, Aaron whispered, "Thank you."

As they walked out of Giovanni's, Jason said, "Now, let's go get some latkes."

CHRISTMAS:
"CHRISTMAS IN THE CITY"
BY PETER SAENZ

I check my cell phone for today's weather forecast: dreary. Always an optimist, I put my best foot forward and get out of bed anyway. I yawn, and stretch as I scratch the middle of my chest, which, to be honest, is getting a bit too many grey hairs for my liking. The warm water from the shower takes me out of my morning haze and into a realm of sweet delight. I then slip into my festive new holiday travel duds. 'Not bad if I do say so myself', I think, looking into a mirror.

As I leave my hotel room, I almost run into a very good looking middle-aged man.

"Sorry.", I say, trying not to be so obviously drawn into his deep green eyes.

Smiling back at me, he says in a husky Australian accent, "No worries. You going out?"

"Yeah. It's Christmas so I'm gonna be traveling a lot in the car today." I reply.

Still smiling, he disappointedly says, "Bummer."

Tossing my scarf around my neck, I say goodbye to the pretty Aussie, and wish him a Merry Christmas. He winks at me before turning to continue down the hall. I bite my lower lip as I see his curvaceous assets slip around the corner and out of sight. Knowing I have a full day ahead of me, I turn the opposite direction with a purpose.

Zooming down Santa Monica Blvd., I don't see as many people out and about. The ghost town ambiance is a bit unnerving but understandable due to it being a major holiday. The emptiness stirs up melancholy feelings in my mind as my thoughts drift to my ex. It's been almost a year since Josh and I broke up, and although I know in my heart that it was the right thing to do, the Christmas season makes it that much harder to repel the inevitable holiday blues.

Turning onto Havenhurst Drive, I park the car and grab the gift I'll need. Passing through the main doors of a large apartment building, I walk by several units filled with Christmas merry making. I laugh out loud when I spot an empty bottle of poppers lying outside one door. I shake my head. Damn queens.

After knocking on the right door, it swings open to reveal my best friend Eric standing in a brightly colored elf suit. His shaggy brown hair falls to the side as he jingles the bells on his pointed slippers for my amusement.

"Oh my god, you're a riot!" I shout, squeezing him tightly. "Merry Christmas, you old cougar."

Releasing our hold, Eric replies back, "Merry Christmas to you too, you old tramp. Now come in before you let all the warm air out."

Entering his living room, I hand off my gift to him and say, "This is for you."

"Aw, you shouldn't have." he coos with false modesty. "Yours is still under the tree. Help yourself."

Heading to Eric's Christmas tree, I spot a shiny red and green present with a tag marked "To: Christina, Love: Mommie Dearest".

As Eric anxiously rips through his colorful gift, I stare at him child-like, waiting for his face to magically light up in Christmas cheer. The expression on his face, however, becomes crest-fallen once he pulls out what's inside.

"A Bette Midler Christmas CD? Really Brad?" The sarcasm in his voice is palpable.

"Open it, you bitter old queen." I bark back. I squeeze my body inward in excitement.

Inside are two 3rd row seats to Bette Midler's concert in Las Vegas, along with a Southwest gift card for good measure.

With a humbled expression, Eric says, "Oh my god, I love it! Thank you SO much!"

Inside of my box I find the latest iPhone model.

"No way!" I gush, ripping apart the packaging.

Eric chimes in with a snide, "You're welcome. Now maybe you'll actually answer your phone when I call you."

The next hour is spent reminiscing about old times and helping Eric pick out the cutest outfit for dinner with his new beau later that night. By the time his grandfather clock next chimes, I'm kissing Eric goodbye on the cheek and waltzing out the door.

When I arrive at my sister's Pasadena home, my nephew and niece come flying out the door, practically tackling me with hugs. They take my bag of gifts and excitedly race them inside. After kissing my sister hello, the two of us sit and watch the kids *Ooo* and *Ahh* over their latest batch of material pleasures. My nephew tells me the video game I got him is his favorite, while my niece coyly says that the girls at school will be completely jealous of her new designer outfit.

As the kids disappear to test out their new gifts, my sister practically injects me with one Martha Stewart recipe after another. By the third entree I tell her that if I have one more bite of anything that I'll explode. She says fine, but ends up packing up at least three plates full of food into the refrigerator to take home with me.

When we sit to let our food settle, my love life instantly becomes an open book as my sister immediately goes into her police interrogation persona. My sister is a lot like my mother in that she feels it's her personal responsibility to make sure I'm a happy little kept wife one day. We're famous for our day later dish and supposition.

With a smile on her face, my sister hands me a small Christmas present. I open it to find my father's wedding ring inside.

My sister tells me, "I know you've always wanted it. I thought about getting you clothes or some new gadget to play with, but I know this would mean a lot more to you."

I can feel the tears welling up in my eyes. "I can't take this. Mom and dad left it to you."

Closing my hand over the ring box, my sister says, "It's yours."

I hold her, telling her, "Thank you."

I wipe my tears away as she opens her gift. Inside she finds a gift certificate for a series of cooking classes at the Los Angeles Cordon Bleu Culinary Academy, and a couple hand written coupons good for one day of babysitting each. Once her dramatic scream is over, she starts gushing on and on about all the wonderful dishes she'll be able to make and how Janet from down the street will have to eat crow at her next dinner party. I just smile and enjoy my sister's moment of bliss with her.

After leaving Pasadena, I travel to the Long Beach ASPCA where I volunteer several times a month, mostly walking dogs and socializing with the cats. Once everyone is walked and fed, I update the main board as complete.

Walking toward the cat room, I pass the general infirmary office and see that there's one patient still left inside. Once in, I see a Siberian Husky looking back at me from behind his prison bars with the saddest sky blue eyes. I lift up the paper tag on his cage door and read: '*New, temporary quarantine, not yet named*'.

"Aw, now who'd ever not want to take care of you?" I ask the dog. His tail thumps against the kennel wall in response.

I place my hand near the cage door. My new furry friend sniffs it for a moment, then proceeds to give my hand, and metal gate between it, a thorough tongue bath. Feeling there is no danger to me; I open the cage door and let the poor guy out. Attempting to lick every inch of my face in gratitude, the Husky lets me know in no uncertain terms that I am loved. I've had my heart stolen by several dogs and cats at the shelter before, but something tells me that I may not be able to walk away from this one so easily.

After socializing with the new stray for a while, I give the dog one last playful bear hug before I entice him back into his kennel with a fresh bowl of kibble. Once in, I walk over to the main desk, take a black marker from the drawer, and cross out '*not yet named*' on the quarantine tag, scribbling in '*Buddy*' underneath it.

My next stop takes me to Silver Lake. Scott's lake view, early century, craftsman home is the envy of all of his friends. So naturally, he makes sure they all come to his yearly Christmas party to enjoy that which they can never truly have. Scott is the friend you love to hate. He'll give any friend in need the shirt off of his back, but will also make sure to gently remind said friend, every so often, exactly where they might have ended up without his help.

Letting myself in, I yell, "Hey Scott! I'm here!" into no room in particular. "I just got back from the shelter." Seeing Scott enter from the kitchen, I pass him his gift and say, "Here's a little prezzi I got for you. If you don't mind, I'm gonna shower and change here."

Scott tells me where the towels are upstairs, but not before silently inspecting my gift's wrapping job in judgment.

Shower two changes my scent of animal fur and doggie chow to the aroma of musky body wash and masculine after shave. Arr, I feel so butch! I'm suddenly slapped back down to reality though, spotting myself in the mirror, primping my hair worse than any queen I've known.

I quickly change into the new outfit in my duffle bag and charge back down the stairs. It doesn't take long before more party goers arrive. The night is filled with lots of hugs, kisses, and the occasional scandalous social faux pas from the slightly inebriated.

When the party activity moves from singing Christmas carols and show tunes around the piano to a more risqué game of Truth or Dare, I quietly slip out onto the back patio so as not to partake in what will undoubtedly become a '*can you believe*' moment for the next several months.

Once I'm outside I'm suddenly confronted with the image of my ex-boyfriend Josh deep in the throes of a passionate kiss with some unknown Latin boy. I freeze in place as my mouth suddenly goes dry. Like a horrific car accident, my eyes and body can't seem to move from viewing the tragic turn of events.

Finally releasing their lip lock in order to breathe, Josh spots me and smiles. "Brad!" he says, extending his arms outward, ready for a hug.

Still frozen with my arms by my side, I answer back, "Josh…I didn't know you'd be here."

Realizing a reciprocal hug will not be forthcoming; Josh puts his arms down and says, "Well, Scott's my friend too. Didn't he tell you he invited me?"

Now flushed, I calmly say, "No, he didn't."

With a big smile, Josh continues, "Well, Merry Christmas Brad. Oh! I'd like you to meet my new friend Paul. Paul, this is my old friend Brad."

Paul naively extends his hand in front of him. "It's really nice to meet you."

In a zombie-like trance I take Paul's hand and weakly shake it. I robotically say back, "I really wish I could stay to learn ALL about you, but Scott needs me in the kitchen."

As if I were suddenly possessed by a will other than my own, I turn-on heal and head back into the house. Whipping by the Truth or Dare group, I squeeze through the kitchen door frame, presently filled by another couple taking advantage of the hanging mistletoe. Once I reach the sink, I grab it for support, taking several deep breaths inward. I feel as if I'm gonna be sick.

"Hey mate, fancy seeing you here."

I turn to see the gorgeous Australian from earlier today, now beautifully dressed in slacks and a sport coat. The dark polo shirt he wears beneath it nicely shows a thatch of hair peaking over the top. I focus on it, hoping the world around me would stop spinning. Still mentally reeling from my previous encounter with my ex, all I can do is smile back weakly.

With a slight look of concern on his face, he asks, "Are you alright?"

I tilt my head to the side, closing my eyes, imagining Josh lying beneath an SUV.

"I'm fine." I tell him. "Wouldn't be one of Scott's Christmas parties without a little drama."

Laughing, the green eyed specimen in front of me extends his hand and says, "Well, whatever it is, I hope it wasn't too bad. I don't think we were ever properly introduced. I'm Dick."

I immediately start coughing, trying to suppress the internal laughter.

"I'm sorry." I reply, taking his hand. "You just caught me off guard. Hi, my name's Brad. Pleased to meet you. So, how do you know Scott?"

"I work for Qantas Airlines." he answers. "I met Scott when he was on holiday in Sydney. He told me that if I ever stopped in L.A. that I should come over and say hello."

I coolly tell Dick, "Well, I'm glad you did. I wasn't sure if I'd see you again."

Dick forms a huge smirk on his face. I look down and see that we're still holding hands. I can feel my face blush. I'm about to apologize for my embarrassing Freudian blunder when he takes my face in hand and kisses me deeply. Suddenly the world no longer exists. I fall into his arms, giving in to his affection. I feel myself floating, no longer able to even feel my legs.

The whole day becomes a series of faint memories. All I can envision is how beautiful our adopted children would be and if Dick wouldn't mind having to walk a Siberian Husky every once in a while.

When we finally end our kiss, I look back into Dick's deep green eyes.

"Merry Christmas Dick.", I tell him, still savoring his taste.

"Merry Christmas Brad.", he answers back, leaning in for more.

Sis, will I ever have a story for you tomorrow.

ABOUT THE AUTHORS

David Berger – A Long Island native, David Berger is a twenty-year teaching veteran, sharing his love of reading, writing, and creativity. Starting with comic books and Greek mythology as a child, he eventually found Wonder Woman, and from that initial love, he became a fan of science fiction and fantasy genres, eventually branching out and writing his own stories. A high school short story turned novel, "*Task Force: Gaea—Finding Balance*" brings together all of David's literary loves into one compelling story, one that will be the springboard for future adventures of his four heroes. A passion second only to teaching, writing allows him the freedom to explore nuanced ideas, redefining the ancient stories he grew up with into new, inspired directions. He currently lives with his partner Gavi in Land O' Lakes, FL with their two cats. **www.taskforce-gaea.com**

Warner Davidson - Warner Davidson currently lives in Washington, DC with his husband and partner of 20 years, Marc Wittlif. His lifelong dream of being a writer remained unrealized until now because ... well, because he was an idiot and kept telling himself that he couldn't do it. Turns out he was wrong. His two contributions to this volume are his first publications. Warner and Marc hope one day soon to put the ugly world of DC politics behind them and relocate to Palm Springs, CA to write and live happily ever after. Until then, they hold their noses and carry on.

Hank Henderson – Hank Henderson is a Los Angeles writer and performer. He studied creative writing at UCLA and Terry Wolverton's Writers at Work. His one man show "*Greetings From the Fugue State*" premiered at the 2010 Queer festival Behold at Highways Performance Space and was part of West Hollywood's 25th Anniversary celebration. Henderson curates the LGBTQI reading series homo-centric. Since January 2010 homo-centric has presented over 220 writers & performers at Stories Books in Echo Park as well as the West Hollywood Book Fair and WeHo's Pride Month. He lives with Joe, his partner of 19 years, in Glassell Park. **www.homo-centric.com**

Salvador Hernandez - Salvador Hernandez is a student of the film department at Santa Fe University in New Mexico. This is his first published story.

Peter Saenz – Peter Saenz spent the majority of his growing years in both Southern California and parts of South Texas. He's always been fascinated with the fantasy genre and is a fan of authors: Anne Rice, David Sedaris, J.K. Rowling and Roald Dahl. Peter's writing has thus far been released in two works: the short story collection "*Queer Tales: A Fantasy Anthology*", which he coordinated; and the solo novel "*Coven of Wolves*". Peter currently lives in Los Angeles with his husband Joseph and their cat Pickles. **www.peterjsaenz. com**

Mitchum Sinclair - Mitchum Sinclair first burst on to the acting scene as Extra #2 in "*The Petrified Forest*" with Bette Davis. He earned raves for his performance as Delivery Man in "*The Women*" with Joan Crawford. His later nightclub act: "*Call Me Mitch*" ran for 2 1/2 weeks at the Coconut Grove and served as a springboard for his afternoon talk show, "*The Mitchum Sinclair Show*". Along with Merv Griffin and Dick Cavett, the show was known as The Place where stars could talk and feel comfortable. The show ran for 3 successful years, until the network was forced to cancel due to the number of sexual harassment claims the male Hispanic production crew filed. Mitchum now spends his time writing, with his partner and his 24 cats in an apartment in WeHo.

Alan Smithee – Writer, director, producer… Alan Smithee has done it all! Probably the most successful and famous person in the group, Alan's long resume of scripts, film, and television work can be found on IMDB. com. Winner of many Razzie Awards, Alan Smithee is a professional in the industry without peer.

Robbie Tursi-Masick – Hailing from the mysterious land of Ronkonkoma in the Island of Long, Robbie grew up dreaming of the day the dark, handsome Mediterranean Prince of his dreams would whisk him away from the boring life he was accustomed to a land far, far away. (Well, far enough away so that his mother couldn't visit on a regular basis.) A magical place full of roller skates and rainbows called Xanadu. But, as with most of these stories, that never happened. He was instead whisked away to Westchester for some time and the "prince" turned out to be a very pale country bumpkin from Schenectady (Yes, it's a real place). While he's not spending the day being a real housewife of Long Island, taking care of his four-legged children, Kira & Carter, Robbie can be found on YouTube performing various 11 O'Clock numbers from Broadway shows like "Gypsy" & "Dreamgirls" and/or annoying his husband, Kevin. Robbie is still waiting to sign off on the adoption papers from Lynda Carter. **www.youtube.com/user/WonderRobbie**

ABOUT THE ARTIST

Jon Macy - Jon was part of the early Nineties black and white art boom with the series *Tropo*. It was followed by the erotic horror comic series *Nefarismo* from Eros/Fantagraphics. Since then he has created strips for gay skin magazines such as *Steam, Wilde, Bunkhouse* and *International Leatherman*, as well as the anthologies *Gay Comix, Negative Burn, Meatmen, Friend of Dorothy, So Super Duper, Three, Glamazonia* and *Boytrouble*. He has also created illustrations for the first *Fallen Angel*, a landmark leather DVD by Titan Media. He is best known for his graphic novel *Teleny and Camille*, an adaptation of the anonymous Victorian novel of gay love attributed to Oscar Wilde and circle which won the prestigious Lambda Literary Award for gay erotica. His most recent work, *Fearful Hunter*, is the recipient of the 2010 PRISM Comics Queer Press Grant. Jon lives in the San Francisco Bay Area and is single. **www.jonmacy.com**

www.ingramcontent.com/pod-product-compliance
Lightning Source LLC
Chambersburg PA
CBHW060549260626
47161CB00003B/1126